D1304773

Lila exhaled. "What is this deal with you not accepting gifts, Mandy? I mean, you should be touched by how much the Unicorns care about you."

"Wait a second," I said slowly. "You want *me* to be happy?"

Suddenly something clicked. "This is some weird conniving way to get me back into the club!"

Lila put her hands on her hips. "So what if it is? We're just showing you that we'd do anything for you. I mean, do you think the Angels would go as far as buying you a house?"

"Of course they wouldn't!" I shouted. "Nobody with a normal sense of values would even consider it."

"But who ever wanted to be normal? We're the Unicorns. We're the best friends you could ever have," Lila pressed.

I stared at her, feeling my eyes fill with tears. "No, you're not. Just because you're rich doesn't mean you're nice people or good friends. So just leave me alone," I said hotly. "Maybe there are a lot of things that your daddy can buy you, Lila, but I'm not one of them!"

Lila reached for my arm. "Mandy, don't be—"

"Don't even try," I told her, jerking my arm away. "I don't want to have anything to do with you. You're shallow and spoiled and totally clueless!"

Bantam Books in THE UNICORN CLUB series.
Ask your bookseller for the books you have missed.

THE UNICORN CLUB™

MANDY IN THE MIDDLE

Written by
Alice Nicole Johansson

Created by
FRANCINE PASCAL

BANTAM BOOKS
NEW YORK · TORONTO · LONDON · SYDNEY · AUCKLAND

To Judy and Alan Adler

RL 4, 008-012

MANDY IN THE MIDDLE

A Bantam Book / March 1996

Sweet Valley High® and The Unicorn Club®
are registered trademarks of Francine Pascal

Conceived by Francine Pascal

Produced by Daniel Weiss Associates, Inc.
33 West 17th Street
New York, NY 10011

Cover art by James Mathewuse

ISBN: 0-553-48355-2
Published simultaneously in the United States and Canada

Bantam Books are published by Bantam Books, a division of Bantam
Doubleday Dell Publishing Group, Inc. Its trademark, consisting of the
words "Bantam Books" and the portrayal of a rooster, is Registered in U.S.
Patent and Trademark Office and in other countries. Marca Registrada.
Bantam Books, 1540 Broadway, New York, New York 10036.

PRINTED IN THE UNITED STATES OF AMERICA

OPM   0 9 8 7 6 5 4 3 2 1

One

"Spare me, Lila," Kimberly Haver groaned as I stepped out of my walk-in closet. "You're not seriously planning on wearing *that*."

"Major misfire," Jessica Wakefield added, looking me over from head to toe.

"What do you mean?" I asked, striking a pose in front of my full-length mirror. The other members of the Unicorn Club and I were putting together outfits for the Earth Day celebration at school the next day. We had been told to dress for the occasion, in hippie garb, or anything else that fit with the theme Save the Planet. "What's wrong with my outfit?"

After all, they were talking to me, Lila Fowler, self-proclaimed clotheshorse and reigning recipient of the Best Dressed award at Sweet Valley Middle School.

"You don't seriously think that pearls count as love beads?" Kimberly teased, tugging at my long antique strand.

Kimberly's never been one to hide what she thinks. Sometimes I think of that as a strength. At other times I see it as a terrible weakness. Like when she's putting me down, for instance.

"And a purple polka-dot blouse doesn't exactly cut it as a tie-dyed T-shirt," Jessica piped in. "That's like trying to substitute linen for burlap, or velvet for velour." She shook her head. "You really need to rethink this."

"Like you're one to talk," I snapped back. "You look like a total preschooler in those braids."

Jessica batted her long eyelashes and sighed faintly. "I guess this earthy look doesn't really do much for me. I look horrible!"

Typical! Jessica is blond and beautiful, the type that looks great in almost everything she puts on. She was obviously fishing for a compliment, which she definitely wasn't going to get from me after that slam about "rethinking" my outfit.

"Well, I heard that some kids are dressing like trees and endangered species and stuff," Ellen Riteman said. She was flopped out on my canopy bed, painting peace signs on her fingernails. "Maybe we could all dress like California Pines and stick branches in our hair."

"Oh, please!" Kimberly exclaimed.

"Really, Ellen," I added. Ellen is our recently

elected club president. Taking over the honored position has somehow made her more eager and confident about spouting her ditzy and spacey suggestions. Maybe there's a medical explanation, but the way I see it, her mind just can't keep up with her mouth. She says things before her brain has time to process how ridiculous they are.

"You couldn't pay me to be seen in public like that," I went on. "Pearl combs belong in this hair, not pinecones." I fluffed my long brown locks.

"I don't see what the problem is," Ellen said defensively. "*I* think it's a great idea, and I'm president now."

"So?" I put my hands on my hips.

"Well, being president means I have extra decision-making power, doesn't it?" she asked.

"Not if it involves damaging our public image," I replied, quoting one of my dad's business mottoes.

I know it may seem mean when we give Ellen a hard time, but it's mostly just because she's such a good target. And trust me, if we really thought she was a major blockhead, we wouldn't have put her in charge.

"OK, fine," Ellen went on. "I have another idea. We can go as Unicorns in honor of the club. Wear white sweats and make horns out of tinfoil."

Kimberly gave her a look. "I don't know, Ellen. Somehow that doesn't sound like it has anything to do with Earth Day."

"Sure, it does," Ellen argued. "I mean, if you

care about the earth, you care about endangered animals, right?"

"Did you just say 'endangered animals'?" I asked.

Ellen looked confused. "Well—yeah. They *are* endangered, aren't they? Or is it extinct?"

I sighed. "Ellen, are you sure you didn't suffer some kind of head trauma when you were a baby? There's no such thing as a Unicorn. It's mythical."

"I knew that." Ellen's face flushed. "I really did."

"Sure you did," Kimberly spouted back. "Anyway, I heard Aaron, Peter, and Bruce are dressing like a recycling center. Aaron's plastics, Peter's glass, and Bruce is paper."

Aaron Dallas, Peter Jeffries, and Bruce Patman are known as three of the biggest catches at school. If you ask me, they could use a few years of maturity, better manners, and cleaner fingernails. But not everyone has such high standards. My friends think the three of them can do no wrong.

"Isn't that what they were for Halloween?" Jessica smiled at the memory.

"That's the cutest part about it," Kimberly explained with admiration. "They've *recycled* their costumes."

Ellen nodded appreciatively. "That is so totally smart."

I don't know if Ellen is the best judge of someone's intelligence, but I had to admit, it *was* a clever idea. "That does sound pretty cute," I agreed.

"We have to think of something cool, too,"

Jessica said, unweaving one of her braids.

I grabbed the phone on my bedside table. "I'll call my dad's tailor and see if he can whip something together."

"Hey, good idea. Maybe he could make us matching suede fringe vests," Kimberly suggested.

"Too bulky," Jessica objected. "How about suede miniskirts with knee-high boots and bolero jackets?"

"He'll never have time to do it by tomorrow morning," I remarked. "He's a tailor, not a miracle worker. I guess we'll just have to make do with the stuff in my closet."

"Why don't we just forget about the hippie look," Kimberly suggested. Ellen untied the leather headband she had strapped around her forehead. "I second that motion."

"Hmm." Jessica clicked her tongue against the roof of her mouth, thinking. A smile suddenly grew on her face. "Maybe . . ."

"Yes?" I prompted her eagerly. Jessica has amazing creative instincts. Maybe she'd thought of the perfect costume for the four of us to wear. Something that would make us stand out. Whenever the Unicorns can make a statement, it's good for club visibility.

"I was just thinking—if I dress all in green in honor of plant life, I'd really bring out the green in my eyes," Jessica told us.

If I dress in green? I thought. What about us? We? The Unicorns? "I thought we were doing this together," I said.

"Well, obviously, we were getting nowhere," Jessica replied. "We might as well each do our own thing."

"That gives me an awesome idea." Ellen's blue eyes lit up. "Blue's always been my best color. And it stands for the sky and ocean." She headed for my chest of drawers. "Mind if I borrow your blue angora sweater, Lila?"

Kimberly tapped her fingers on my dresser. "You know, that reminds me . . . hey, Lila, where's that killer yellow cardigan with the matching mini-skirt? That could represent the sun."

"That outfit's brand new," I told her. "I haven't worn it yet."

"And we all know that life on Earth wouldn't even exist if we didn't have the sun," Kimberly went on.

I cleared my throat. "Yeah, well—"

"And we *also* know how amazingly awesome I look in yellow," Kimberly added, smiling brightly.

"I hope you didn't send your green silk pants to the dry cleaner, Lila," Jessica called out from my closet.

"My green silk pants?" I repeated. "Actually, I was planning to wear those on—"

"Oh, score. Here they are," she broke in.

". . . Friday," I continued flatly.

"Chill out, Lila," Jessica replied. "You'll have them back by then."

"Yeah—crumpled and stained," I muttered.

Jessica may have an eye for selecting fine clothes, but she doesn't exactly have a knack for taking care of them.

"This is totally gorgeous." Kimberly snipped the price tags off the yellow outfit I was saving for a special occasion.

I bit my lip as I watched my friends dress up in my clothes. I'm normally generous about lending things, but somehow it was bugging me.

"So what am I supposed to dress in?" I asked. "Brown for the dirt?"

"Are these flattering?" Jessica asked the mirror.

I cleared my throat. "You guys are all wearing my stuff. Can't you at least help me out in return?"

"Oh, you'll think of something," Ellen said flippantly. "Now. If I wear jeans and blue sneakers, do you think people will know I'm sky, or should I wear a sign that says I am?"

"Is this a good tone of yellow for me?" Kimberly asked, modeling my cashmere cardigan. "It might be too bright. Maybe I should take up my mom's offer to get my colors done."

"Oh, yeah, that shade overpowers you," I said, trying to sound persuasive. "Maybe *I* should wear my brand-new outfit and be the sun, and *you* should think of something else to wear."

Jessica snapped her fingers. "I have a better idea."

"Do tell," I replied, hoping that this time it would include me.

"I'll dress like a rainbow. Wear rainbow suspenders and different color ribbons in my hair," Jessica said, fishing through my basket of hair accessories. "Of course I'll wear a purple skirt and top. The coolest color in the entire rainbow."

Purple is our official club color, and I'm not the only one who has a closet stuffed with purple everything. But by this point I *was* the only one without an outfit for tomorrow. "So should I wear green?" I asked hesitantly. I loved my silk pants and everything, but I didn't exactly like the idea of dressing in the clothes Jessica had rejected.

"Would blue eye shadow be too much?" Ellen wondered.

"You know, if you really look closely, I think this shade enhances my tan," Kimberly declared, carefully reexamining the sweater against her olive skin.

I shook my head furiously. No one was listening to anyone. Sometimes my friends can get so self-absorbed, it drives me crazy. I mean, sometimes they say the same thing about me, but believe me, it's different.

"Maybe I just won't wear any clothes at all. It'll represent my return to nature," I said, testing to see if I'd get a response.

"You know what would be cute with this?" Kimberly asked, staring at her reflection. "Those gold daisy earrings we were looking at."

"You mean the ones Mandy's been dying for?" Ellen asked.

"She was practically drooling over them in the store," Jessica recalled. "Too bad they were so expensive."

Hearing Mandy Miller's name made me miss her like crazy. Mandy is giving, thoughtful, and funny—not to mention a fabulous dresser. Until recently she was a member of the Unicorn Club.

"I wish Mandy were here," I sighed softly. "I wish she were still a Unicorn."

Ellen bit her lip. "Yeah," she said wistfully.

"It's just too hard to believe that she could actually bail on us," Kimberly commented. "Who wouldn't want to be part of the coolest club in school?"

"Apparently Mandy," Ellen responded.

"Well, the Unicorn Club just doesn't feel the same without her," Jessica admitted.

She was right about that. The Unicorn Club has actually undergone a ton of changes since the beginning of the school year. First of all, we lost a lot of members (including our founding president, Janet Howell) when they became freshmen at Sweet Valley High. And then our first battle over who should take over the presidency began. To me it was obvious. I have all the skills it takes to keep a group running efficiently and all the role models a girl could ask for. My dad owns Fowler Enterprises, the most successful business in Sweet Valley, and I've always paid close attention to his organization tactics. Plus, Janet is my cousin and had been grooming me to take over the role all last year. But Jessica didn't see it that way. She was positive that the presidency belonged to her and was willing to do almost anything to get me to back down. In the midst of a dare war, Jessica and I realized that there was an even more qualified candidate. Mandy Miller.

Under Mandy's leadership, the Unicorns seemed better than ever. We did everything we could to bring out the best in each other and we even invited some new, more diverse, members into the club: Jessica's mentally opposite, but physically identical, twin, Elizabeth; Elizabeth's best friend, Maria Slater; and Evie Kim, a sixth grader who was new at school.

Things ran smoothly . . . for a few weeks. That was until everyone took sides during student body elections, and half of the club formed a new group called the Angels. I can't say losing Elizabeth or Maria or Evie has impacted the quality of our club. I mean, they did get us into volunteering at the day-care center, and helped us out a lot during fund-raisers and stuff, but if you ask me, those girls are a little too goody-goody for our tastes.

But Mandy is another story. You see, Mandy's been on the fence about which club she feels she belongs with. For some bizarre reason, lately she's been leaning toward the Angels. Of course, an organization can't be headed by a person who's not a full-fledged member. So once we realized that Mandy was wavering, we knew we had to pick another president. Finally I thought my time had come. Unfortunately, so did Jessica. And Kimberly. The only one who wasn't fighting for the presidency was Ellen. And we decided that she was really the best choice of all. In a lot of ways, Ellen is the backbone of the group. She may seem a little dense, but when it comes down to it, she'll do anything for the club. And her mom makes these killer desserts when the meetings are at her house. But even though Ellen's a great president, I can't help missing Mandy.

"Has anyone been noticing how Mandy's rushed off every day after school?" Ellen said.

I nodded. "She won't even stop to tell me where she's going."

"I bet she's been putting in a lot of time at the day-care center," Kimberly guessed.

"Mandy's always volunteering her time for something," I said with admiration. "She's really into this rain forest thing, I think."

"Well, Elizabeth told me that the Angels have been volunteering at the library after school," Jessica chimed in.

"What a bunch of losers!" Kimberly added snippily.

"Mandy must be with them, updating the card catalog or something useless," Ellen said regretfully just as the grandfather clock in the living room began to chime.

"Oh, my gosh!" Kimberly shrieked. "Is it four already? I told Jake that I'd watch his football practice. I'd better bolt."

Jake Hamilton is a gorgeous eighth grader, a star athlete, and Kimberly's latest conquest.

"He looks so incredible in his jersey," Kimberly gushed as she quickly folded my yellow outfit and slid it into her patent leather backpack.

I felt a surge of irritation. "That's cashmere, Kimberly. At least take it in a hanging bag."

"It'll be fine, Lila," she said, ducking out of the room. "Catch you later."

Ellen turned to Jessica. "We'd better get a move on, too. Aaron and Rick are probably already waiting for us at Casey's."

"Wait a second," I protested. "Why did you guys come over if you had something else to do?"

"Because we needed something to wear tomorrow," Jessica said matter-of-factly, shoving a bunch of ribbons into her lavender backpack.

I folded my arms. "Well, gee, it's nice to know that I can be of service to you."

"Yeah, now I'll have a killer outfit," Jessica said, changing back into her school clothes.

"I'm really psyched to be the sky," Ellen added, dropping my blue clothes into a pile on the floor.

"Um, aren't you guys forgetting something?" I asked, staring at the messy pile.

Jessica looked at me in the mirror as she played with her hair. "What? Do you think I should wear a headband? Maybe I should borrow your black velvet one. . . ."

"That's *not* what I meant," I grumbled. Then I took a deep breath and smiled sweetly. "Listen, you guys," I said in my most charming voice, "I have a great idea. Why don't you help me clean up, and then we can all go down to Casey's—"

"Actually, could I borrow this lavender satin headband instead?" Jessica asked, grabbing it off my dresser and flinging her backpack over her shoulder.

"See you later, Lila," Ellen sang out as she and Jessica sailed through the door.

"Whatever," I muttered to myself as they disappeared from my view.

I heard them giggling as they headed down the staircase.

I gritted my teeth and looked around my room. Snack plates and soda cans littered the floor. Magazines were strewn over the bed. My mirrored closet was smeared with fingerprints and lipstick smudges. Ellen hadn't even bothered to put the tops on the nail polish bottles. My friends had turned my room inside out and upside down and actually had the nerve to leave without offering to help clean it up.

I sighed and did the smartest thing a girl in my situation could do: I hit the intercom button that connects me with the maid's room.

"Mrs. Pervis?" I asked. "Could you give me a hand up here?"

*   *   *

A live-in housekeeper is one of the many benefits I get from having the richest dad in town. I don't know where Mrs. Pervis got her special touch, but by the time I'd hung up my clothes, she had whizzed around the room with a vacuum, a garbage bag, and some glass cleaner and restored it to its original state.

According to a recent article in *Architectural Design*, our mansion is "a magnificent demonstration of elegance with a touch of modernism." And I agree that there are some pretty amazing things here: like the black-bottomed pool, the screening room, and the art deco furniture in the basement. But to me, nothing is more wonderful than my bedroom. I decorated it in lavender and cream tones. My canopy bed is fit for a queen, covered with lacy blankets and goose down throw pillows. I have a love seat in the corner patterned with pink and yellow tulips. An awesome stereo system and wide-screen TV sit on my entertainment unit beneath my collection of all my favorite Johnny Buck movies.

Sometimes I think I could just live in my room, without bothering to go to the kitchen or the living room. I could have Jean Luc, our chef, bring me my meals.

Of course, I'd still leave the house for school, parties, shopping, and Unicorn meetings. Charles, our chauffeur, is always available to take me wherever I need to go.

I know my life might sound pretty enviable, but it has its downside, too. You see, my parents got divorced when I was a little girl, and my mom's lived in Europe ever since. And the biggest bummer about my dad's job is that it takes so much of his time. Sometimes he doesn't come home from the office until nine at night and he constantly has to go out of town on business trips. This week he's in New York. As you may imagine, it can get pretty lonely around here.

This is why I've always valued the Unicorn Club so much. They're like my extended family. I'm always going to Jessica's for dinner. Kimberly's mom makes a special point of inviting me to spend holidays with them when she knows my dad is traveling. And now that Ellen's parents are divorced, we've spent a lot of time talking about how it makes us feel. It's brought us even closer together.

But every once in a while there are days like today, when the Unicorns disappoint me. It was rude of them to leave without offering to clean up. And they should have told me they had other plans before they took up my offer to come over after school. Plus, it was selfish of them not to bother helping me pick out an outfit for Earth Day, especially after they acted like wild scavengers picking through my wardrobe.

I got up and took one last walk through my closet. What could I wear tomorrow? I had a great outfit to wear for my dad's upcoming yacht christening, a gorgeous dress for the next school dance, and this beautiful flowered sarong that I was saving for my next trip to the beach. But for Earth Day? Nothing. I had nothing.

Forget it, I decided. I'd rather not dress up at all than wear something that wasn't special. I could just tell everyone that the Earth Day theme was a little immature for Lila Fowler.

I plopped on my bed and reached for the bottle of clear nail polish. *If only Mandy were here*, I thought. She has the most creative sense of style I've ever seen. She buys most of her clothes at thrift stores and manages to look like a million bucks.

But that's not what I missed most about her. Mandy is incredibly thoughtful. She never would have left my room in a mess to go hang out with some guys.

In a way, it's weird that I miss her so much. I mean, at first I was totally opposed to Mandy's becoming a Unicorn. I didn't think she was pretty or popular enough. And now here I am, not even a year later, ready to beg Mandy to come back. She isn't the prettiest girl at school, and she obviously isn't the richest, but the truth is that somewhere along the way, Mandy Miller became the heart and soul of the Unicorn Club.

I strummed my fingers on my bedside table. There had to be a way to change Mandy's mind. There had to be a way to convince her that she belonged with the Unicorns.

It was at that very moment that I made a personal pledge to myself: to recruit Mandy Miller back into the Unicorn Club, whatever it took. As I've learned from my dad, a Fowler doesn't ever take no for an answer.

Two

"I spy with my little eye, something that begins with *W*," I said.

I was in the cancer wing of the Sweet Valley Children's Hospital, playing a game of I spy with Randall Everett Boyer III. Randall was under the covers of his bed, wearing the purple baseball cap that I had given him last week. He's been pretty shy about showing his head since he lost all his curly red hair from chemotherapy. You see, Randall's suffering from bone cancer. He's only seven.

"Is it the window, Mandy?" he asked, looking around the room.

I shook my head. "Negative."

"The wall?" he asked.

"You're warm," I told him. "Very toasty."

"The wall*paper*!" he exclaimed.

I smiled. "Bingo. I'm glad they put up this clown wallpaper. When I was here, the walls were plain white."

"Boring!" Randall wrinkled his nose.

I rolled my eyes. "You're telling *me*."

You see, I was in the hospital a year ago. I had cancer, too. A kind called non-Hodgkin's lymphoma. Like Randall, I went through surgery, chemotherapy, and radiation treatments. Every last strand of my reddish-brown waist-length hair fell out from the chemo, and it's taken me a year to grow it back past my shoulders. But stuff like hair becomes sort of trivial when you're really sick. You don't need it to survive. Besides good doctors, the stuff you need is love and attention and a distraction from all the pain. I'll never forget how well I was treated by the hospital staff and how happy I was when a candy striper named Ami made her special visits to see me.

That's why, when I recovered, I promised myself that I'd give something back to someone else with cancer. For a while, the thought of stepping back into this place made my stomach queasy. But recently I decided it was time to push aside my fears and give it a go. My first day volunteering I met Randall. I've been back every afternoon since.

"My turn," Randall said. "I spy with my little eye . . . something that begins with M.M."

"M.M.?" I scratched my head, pretending to be

stumped. "Let's see. Is it . . . a makeup mirror?"

Randall crossed his arms over his chest. "Nope."

"A mucous membrane?"

"What's that?" Randall looked disgusted.

I giggled. "Just something I learned in biology. You'll learn all about it in about . . . six years."

"Six years?" He widened his eyes. "Guess that means you think I'm gonna get better."

"It's a sure thing," I replied.

Randall's doctors say that his chance of a full recovery is excellent. The tumor in his leg grew back after his first operation a year ago, but they're confident that after his surgery next week and continued doses of chemo, he'll be good as new. They've told me it's important to assure Randall that if he fights hard, there's no reason he can't live to be one hundred and one.

"Well? Do you give up?" Randall challenged, his green eyes looking out from under the brim of the baseball cap.

"Hey, wait a second." I tilted my head. "Is it me? Mandy Miller?"

"Yup." He giggled.

"That was a good one, Randall," I said.

He smiled proudly. "Hey, guess what, Mandy? Four more days till I get to see my mom again." He pointed to the little countdown chart drawn with crayons beside his bed.

The hardest part about Randall's treatment is that he has to be separated from his mom during the week. There's a hospital much closer to his home in northern California, but the facilities and doctors in Sweet Valley are considered the best in the state. If Randall's mom could, she'd be here every day. But her boss says she can't keep taking so much time off. And so she drives all the way down after work on Friday and returns late Sunday so that she can report back to work on Monday.

"I wish there was a way she could live here with me. Maybe they could put a special bed in the corner," Randall said hopefully. "I'd even let her watch those dumb talk shows she likes instead of cartoons."

I blinked my eyes, trying to hide my sadness. "But your mom has to go to work. She needs the money to support you guys and the health insurance that pays for all your medical care," I explained. "So you have to be a big boy and show your mom that you can be really strong without her."

"I guess," he sighed.

A candy striper leaned into the room. "Visiting hours are over," she announced. "Sorry."

"Already?" Randall complained.

She nodded and ducked back out.

I checked the wall clock, which read six o'clock. I couldn't believe all the time that had passed! I still had to do my homework, throw together an outfit for the Earth Day celebration tomorrow, and help my mom with dinner. Lately I'd blown off a lot of things to be here for Randall, but there were certain responsibilities I couldn't avoid.

"Please don't go," Randall pleaded, grasping onto my hand.

I gave his hand a squeeze. "I'll be back tomorrow. I promise. And we can play whatever you want."

Randall frowned. Our partings always went something like this. I never let on how hard it was for *me* to leave *him*.

"Checkers," I said cheerfully. "We'll play checkers. I'll even let you be red."

"You always let me be red," he reminded me.

I grinned. "Yeah, well, tell you what. I'll also let you use my special drawing pencils."

His eyes looked hopeful. "Cool!"

I raised my eyebrows. I didn't realize that colored pencils were *that* alluring. "Well, I guess they're pretty great for drawing intricate designs."

"No, not the pencils." Randall laughed. "I mean, no offense. I just got a great idea."

I looked at him suspiciously. "What?"

Randall leaned toward me and whispered in my ear. "You could hide in here. The nurses would never ever know if you just slide under the bed when they come to check on me. And I'll share my meals with you."

"Hmm. You think that'll work?" I looked under the bed. "Looks pretty uncomfortable down there."

Randall gazed at me with his irresistible puppy-dog eyes. "Pleeeeease?"

I swallowed. He sure wasn't making this any easier. "I'll be back before you know it. You'll probably get sick of seeing me so much. You'll be saying, 'Oh, no, it's Mandy Miller again! Gross!'"

"Never," he said glumly as I slowly moved for the door.

"See you later, alligator." I put on my biggest smile and waved to him as I left the room.

But my smile instantly faded. I couldn't stand the thought of him being in that room all alone. He was only seven, so scared about being sick, so lonely without his mother nearby. His dad died a few years ago, so his mom was practically his whole family. I knew his recovery would be easier if she were around.

I headed down the corridor past the nurses and doctors. When I reached the street, I wiped away a few tears and began my long walk home.

Three

"I could have an information overload," Kimberly complained to me as we walked around the cafeteria together.

It was early afternoon, and classes were over for the day. Earth Day activities were in full swing. The picnic tables had been moved out to make room for booths dedicated to every environmental cause you've ever heard of.

We approached a row of tables set aside for fund raising. The Angels had a table full of homemade organic sweets. A sign above the table announced they were donating their profits to the Rain Forest Foundation. I was sorry to see that Mandy was with them, in charge of the cash box.

"Can you believe Mandy's with the Angels?" Kimberly said, stopping a few tables away from the Angels. "What does she see in them?"

"Tell me about it." I sighed. "I'm at a total loss."

"Did you check out how cute her outfit is?" Kimberly went on.

I studied Mandy's multicolored tie-dyed T-shirt and rust suede miniskirt. She looked adorable. She had even woven fresh flowers into her braids. "It's Mandy Miller. What do you expect?"

Kimberly poked me in the ribs. "Let's find out about solar heating."

"You?" I responded. "The Queen of the electric blanket?"

Kimberly motioned toward a booth. A gorgeous older guy with wavy blond hair was talking to students and handing out brochures. "Shall we?" Kimberly said slyly.

Normally, I'd be the first to take advantage of a gorgeous guy-meeting opportunity, but somehow there was something more important on my mind—talking to Mandy. Judging from her position at the cash box, her commitment to the Angels was stronger than ever. If I didn't do something fast, we might lose her forever. "Go ahead without me," I told Kimberly.

"Your loss." She quickly applied a coat of red lipstick. "How do I look?"

"Great. And I'm sure he'll be charmed that you're dressed as the sun," I pointed out.

She smiled confidently and strutted over to him.

I tossed back my shoulders and took a deep breath. Operation Win Mandy Back was about to begin.

*   *   *

"It is so noble of you guys to do this for the rain forests. If there's any environmental cause that I think needs assistance, this is it," I said passionately, planting myself in front of the Angels' table.

Mandy looked at me suspiciously. "I didn't even know you *knew* about the rain forests."

I cleared my throat. "Yeah, well, I haven't followed it too closely lately, but I know that whatever *is* happening, it's devastating."

Mandy nodded. "You have no idea. Each year, twenty-seven million acres are destroyed. If we don't try to help, by the year 2000, eighty percent of them may be gone. Kaput. *Finito.*"

"Wow, that's rough," I said sympathetically. It was obvious that the fund-raiser meant a lot to Mandy. Playing up my interest could only work in my favor. "So how are sales?"

"Not too hot," Elizabeth admitted, fidgeting with her long strand of love beads.

Mandy shook her head with disappointment. "I was really hoping we could make a bigger contribution."

"Contribution?" I repeated slyly. That was it! A contribution to the Rain Forest Foundation was a sure way to show Mandy my generous nature and score some points on behalf of the Unicorns.

"Yeah, the foundation is going to be bummed," Evie added. She was dressed as a tree, in brown pants, a green turtleneck, and earrings made of leaves.

"I guess not too many students are into eating

sugar-free granola cakes," Mary Wallace pointed out. Mary was one of the original Unicorns who defected to the Angels when the club split up. "Maybe we should sell them for half price."

"Wait a second. Did you say sugar-free granola cakes? I love those." I eyed the cakes, which looked like rabbit food. "My mouth is watering just looking at them."

Mandy wrinkled her nose. "I thought you were into chocolate éclairs and mousse and cheesecake," she said.

I waved my hand dismissively. "Well, that stuff's fine every now and then. But I'm learning how important it is to nourish yourself with wholesome, organic treats like granola cakes." I rubbed my stomach. "I'll take them all."

"All?" Mandy exclaimed.

I wet my lips. "Why not? They look delicious."

"Does Jessica know you like these so much?" Elizabeth asked as she filled up a brown bag with my purchase. "She said she'd rather eat lima beans."

"She just hasn't acquired a taste for them yet," I replied. "I'll help her see the light."

"You should freeze the ones you don't eat right away," Mary suggested. "We didn't use any preservatives, so they could harden up pretty fast."

As far as I was concerned, these babies were heading straight for the nearest trash can. "I doubt they'll last a day."

"Don't eat too many at once," Evie warned.

"They may be a little hard on your digestion."

"It'll take a lot of willpower, but I'll try." I handed over a ten-dollar bill. "Keep the change." I caught Mandy's eyes. "As a matter of fact, here's an extra five."

Mandy raised an eyebrow. "Are you sure about this, Lila?"

I placed my hand on my chest. "If it saves one branch from being massacred, it's worth it to me."

"That's so cool of you," Evie said gratefully. "This more than doubles our sales."

I smiled at them. "Think nothing of it. It's a tax write-off."

"And now that we've gotten rid of inventory, who wants to go check out that battery-operated sports car?" Evie asked.

Mary grimaced. "We've got to clean up the table first."

"You guys go ahead. I'll do it," Mandy offered.

"We can't let you do all the cleanup by yourself," Evie told her.

"No, really, you guys," I said quickly, psyched to have found an opportunity to talk one-on-one with Mandy. "I'll help Mandy."

"Really?" Mandy sounded surprised.

I put on my sweetest smile and nodded. "You guys should see the car. It's not to be believed."

Evie shrugged. "Let's go before they change their minds."

Mary, Evie, and Elizabeth walked away. Finally Mandy and I were alone.

"This is cool of you, Lila," Mandy said, shaking out the tablecloth. "Thanks."

"What can I say?" I replied breezily. "Anything to help out a friend."

Mandy smiled. "Hey, why didn't you dress up for Earth Day?"

I glanced down at my outfit—black leggings, a blazer, and ankle boots. "I had a little trouble thinking of something to wear."

"Then you should have called me. I have tons of this stuff up in our attic." Mandy began wiping the table off with paper towels. "I could have turned you into a totally jivin' hippie chick."

I felt a rush of excitement. If Mandy was willing to take the time to dress me up, she obviously still thought of me as a close friend. And as a close friend, why *wouldn't* she want to be in the club I belonged to? It was time to take Operation Win Mandy Back a step further.

"Come to Casey's after school with us," I offered.

She squinted her eyes. "Well, I'm supposed to be somewhere by three."

"Oh, come on. When was the last time you hung out with all of us?" I asked.

Mandy bit her lip. "I don't know. It's been awhile, hasn't it?"

"Way too long," I replied. "Can't you just get there at three-thirty or something?"

"I don't know, I . . . I shouldn't be late," she said hesitantly.

I looked at her intently. She was being pretty stubborn, but I wasn't going to back down. Didn't she realize that Lila Fowler didn't take *no* for an answer? "It's important to have balance in your life, Mandy. Appointments, homework, *friends*. . . . Just stop by for half an hour." I gave her my best wide-eyed, pleading look. "Please?"

"Well . . ." Mandy said slowly.

"You really deserve it, Mandy," I continued. "You've been working so hard. I mean, putting so much thought into this booth, not to mention that killer outfit. . . ."

Mandy giggled. "And these killer earrings," she said, touching the long, dangly beads. "The backs have been totally killing my ears."

I smiled mischievously. "Just your ears' way of telling you they need fourteen-karat gold. *And* a yummy Casey's break with your friends."

Mandy sighed. "Well, gold's out of the question until I win the lottery, but I guess I could deal with one of those fudge brownie explosions."

"Awesome! I'll see you there." I walked away, purposely leaving my purchase of baked goods behind.

"Thanks for helping me clean up," she called after me.

I grinned contentedly. Everything was going according to plan. Once she was sitting there with the four of us, pigging out on ice cream, talking about old times and upcoming Unicorn outings, we would be hard to resist. If only I could find a way to have some extra pull. A way to show Mandy how important she was to us. Not bribery, of course, but something that would sway her decision.

"Lila?" Mandy called after me.

I turned around.

She held up the brown bag. "You forgot your granola cakes."

"Oh, right. Thanks," I said, running back and reaching for the unwanted sack.

"See you at Casey's," she added, pulling the earrings out of her ears.

"We'll be waiting for you," I promised, watching her slip the earrings into a pouch in her backpack.

"I'm giving up on these things," she sighed.

Something suddenly clicked. "Really?" I raised my eyebrows ever so slightly. As luck would have it, I had stumbled upon the perfect opportunity to change Mandy's mind. Yes, make that a *golden* opportunity.

I scanned the window display at The Gold Rush, a jewelry store on the top level of the Valley Mall. There were ruby and emerald rings, diamond bracelets, and gold watches. Finally I spotted what I was looking for. A delicate pair of daisy-shaped earrings. The very earrings that Mandy had been admiring ever since we noticed them together months ago.

"I'd like the daisy earrings," I told the jewel-adorned salesgirl as I stepped inside. "The small pair in the back."

She looked at me dubiously. "The ones in the *lux-*

ury case, you mean? They're fourteen-karat gold."

"They'd better be," I replied in my snootiest tone. You see, sometimes salespeople don't expect a thirteen-year-old to be making such extravagant purchases. I'm used to this protocol, so I don't take it too personally. I just make sure to let them know who they're dealing with. "Could you put them in a gift box? I'm in a rush."

The girl raised an eyebrow. "Don't you need to know how much they cost?"

"They're for a special friend. Money is no object," I said, pulling out my platinum charge card.

When I placed it on the glass counter, her eyes caught my name at the bottom. We Fowlers are sort of a legend around town. There's a joke that our purchases at Leather, Etc. . . . have put the owner's kids through college.

Her face lit up. "Well then, *Lila*," she said. "Can I interest you in anything else today? I just unpacked a new shipment from Italy."

"Well . . . it's hard for me to say no when we're talking about a sound investment like jewelry." I looked at the display set up behind her. "The Italians have such an eye for design. My father has brought me some wonderful pieces from Milan."

"Oh, how lovely!" she exclaimed. "Milan!"

A gorgeous gold necklace caught my eye. It was a thin chain link with a dainty emerald-cut diamond hanging from it. I was about to ask to try it on when I remembered I had no time to waste.

Mandy would be at Casey's any minute. "Actually, just the earrings today," I said. "I'll be back this weekend to do some real damage."

"Be sure to ask for Janine," she said politely, handing me her card.

I signed off on the sales slip, clutched the little velvet box in my hands, and hurried off. I couldn't wait to see the look in Mandy's eyes when I presented her with the gift. She would be stunned, flattered, touched—in two words: won over. Mandy's return to the club was now a sure thing. By tomorrow she'd be wearing her purple jacket to school and hosting the after-school meeting at her house.

"So here's the deal," I told my friends, as I joined them in our regular booth at Casey's ice cream parlor. "Mandy should be here any minute. If we play our cards right, we'll be able to get her back in the club."

"Really?" Ellen exclaimed hopefully.

"But it's crucial that we say all the right things. We have to show Mandy how much we admire her," I said. "Once we've made her feel totally wanted and everything, I'll take over."

"What about me?" Ellen complained. "I'm president now. Shouldn't I?"

I shook my head. "Mandy has always looked up to me." Then again, who wouldn't?

"She looks up to me, too!" Jessica argued. "And I was friends with Mandy way before you were."

I sniffed and tossed my hair behind my shoulders. Why does everything have to turn into a contest between me and Jessica? I mean, maybe Jessica and Mandy were friends first, but clearly I'm the one who cares the most about getting her back in the club. "Like it or not, Jessica, I'm taking over because I bought her those daisy earrings from The Gold Rush," I explained forcefully.

"Why didn't I think of that?" Ellen wondered, staring out into space.

"Because they're out of your price range," I reminded her. "If anyone wants to pay me for them, then they can have the honor."

"I wish, but they're out of my price range," Ellen said, as if this had just occurred to her.

"OK, fine." Jessica curled her upper lip. "You're in charge."

"As I suspected." I crossed my hands on the tabletop. "Now. When the moment is right, I'm going to present the earrings to Mandy. I think that should show her how much she means to us."

"Mandy will be really touched," Ellen said.

"That *was* pretty good thinking, Lila," Jessica admitted reluctantly.

"Shhh. There she is," Kimberly whispered.

"Mandy! Over here." Jessica signaled to her.

Ellen scooted over and made room in the booth.

"Hey, guys," Mandy said as she approached us.

"I'm so glad you came." I put on my most inviting smile and looked fondly at Mandy.

"It's amazing to see you," Ellen told her, beaming. "As always."

"You, too," Mandy replied halfheartedly as she sat down next to Ellen.

I could tell Mandy felt a little uneasy, probably because she hadn't hung out with all of us in a while. I knew it was my job to make her feel at home.

"Your hair is getting so long," I said. "It's practically back down to your waist."

Mandy smiled. "It's getting there."

"You totally had the coolest outfit at school today, Mandy," Ellen put in.

"Too bad there wasn't a contest," I added. "You'd have scored first place for sure."

"She certainly wouldn't have had any competition from you," Jessica teased, motioning toward my black attire.

I glared at Jessica. Who was she to tease *me*, when she had pranced around all day with *my* hair ribbons and *my* accessories? But this was no time to fight over it. I had to focus on Mandy. "As usual, Mandy, you stood out from the crowd."

"Actually I thought Lois Waller did," Kimberly said with a smirk.

Lois Waller is the fattest girl in our school and the butt of many jokes.

"She's such a major porker," Jessica scoffed. "Wouldn't you just die to know exactly what she eats every day?"

"Probably ten gallons of ice cream." Ellen

puffed up her cheeks. "And that's just breakfast."

"I still can't believe she had the nerve to dress as a whale," Kimberly continued.

"At least she has a sense of humor about herself," Mandy said, defending her. "And any way to raise awareness about the brutal way that whales are slaughtered is positive."

"She definitely raised my *awareness*." Jessica giggled.

Kimberly leaned back in the booth. "You know, I don't know about you guys, but I think all that preaching about saving the planet was worth it just to get a half day."

"Anything to spend less time in the math torture chamber," Jessica agreed.

"But the stuff at those booths seemed like a total waste, too. I mean, who even cares about things like acid rain? It never even rains here anyway," Ellen pointed out.

Mandy frowned. "This kind of stuff *is* really important, you guys."

"Yeah, yeah," Kimberly chimed in, "like I'm really going to get my mom to say no to those plastic bags at the grocery store. They're so much easier to carry than those stupid paper bags."

"Oh, and what's this compost heap thing?" Jessica asked.

"It's sick. You like let your garbage get moldy and use it for fertilizer," Kimberly explained.

"I know it sounds gross, but it cuts down the

amount of waste being dumped into landfills,"
Mandy said seriously. "My sister and I made one in
our backyard. And you may not realize it now, but
if we aren't careful, the environment is going to be
screwed by the time we have grandchildren."

I shifted in my seat. I could see that we had of-
fended Mandy. "You're right, Mandy. We were all
just joking," I said. I didn't want us to come off as
uncaring polluters with bad attitudes. Mandy would
never want to be associated with us if she thought
that was the trademark of our club. I kicked Jessica
under the table. "Weren't we, Jessica?"

Jessica's eyes sparkled with sudden understand-
ing. "You know us—total jokers," she filled in eagerly. "I actually feel pretty passionately about all
the things I learned today. I spent a lot of time at
this water conservation booth and I've decided to
give the three-minute shower guideline a try tomorrow morning."

"You?" Mandy said. "You'd really do that?"

Jessica tossed her silky hair over her shoulders.
"Just don't tease me if my hair looks brittle or something. I may not have time to get all the shampoo out."

"So what'll it be?" a waitress asked as she ap-
peared in front of our table.

We'd had this waitress before. She's at least fifty
years old, wears a big bouffant and, as I recall, has
very little patience for her teenage customers.

Mandy started digging for change at the bottom
of her backpack.

"The usual," Ellen said with a flourish.

"You don't have a usual," I responded.

The waitress rolled her eyes.

"Oh, right. A double of mint chip in a dish with hot butterscotch," Ellen decided. "From now on, that'll be my usual. But, I don't know, then again, it could get boring to always have the same thing every . . ."

"And you?" the waitress asked Mandy, cutting Ellen off.

"Could you give me a second?" Mandy asked, counting a handful of pennies and nickels.

The waitress fanned her face with her order pad.

"Well, I'll take a root beer float," Jessica said.

"Ditto on that," Kimberly added.

"Two root beer floats," the waitress repeated, copying down our order.

"Oh. But make mine with chocolate chip ice cream instead of vanilla," Kimberly informed her.

"Oooh. Sounds good. I'll take chocolate chip, too," Jessica decided.

"Let's see." Mandy grabbed the menu from the center of the table and began to scan the prices of each item. "I guess I'll . . . I'll just take a small soda," she said glumly.

"Actually, cancel that," I said suddenly, smiling at Mandy.

"We'll both have triple fudge brownie explosions with extra whipped cream."

The waitress rolled her eyes and forcefully drew a line through her pad.

"I can't." Mandy blushed and looked at the waitress. "I'm a little low on funds."

The waitress gritted her teeth.

"Don't worry about it, Mandy," I told her. "It's on me."

She widened her eyes. "Are you sure?" she asked shyly.

"She's sure," the waitress said in frustration, dashing away from us.

"Thanks, Lila, this tastes too good to be true," Mandy said, once the waitress had returned with our order. "I'll never have room for dinner. Or breakfast."

"For me, this *is* dinner," I said. "My dad's in New York for another week, and Jean Luc is taking some vacation time."

Mandy stared into her dish. "Well, if you really analyze the ingredients, it covers a lot of food groups. Dairy from the ice cream, bread from the brownie, and even a small portion of fruit." Mandy dangled her maraschino cherry between her fingers.

"Good point. Next time I tell my mom I want sundaes for dinner, I'll have a good argument to back it up," Jessica said appreciatively.

"Just be sure to invite me over that night," Mandy replied.

We all cracked up. It was obvious that Mandy was having a blast with us. I knew the time had come. It was the perfect moment to present her with my gift.

As my dad would say, it would seal the deal.

I reached into my backpack, pulled out the little velvet box, and handed it to her.

Mandy looked confused.

"It's a little present. For you," I said, placing it in front of her.

Her face flushed. "Me?"

I smiled widely. "Go ahead. Open it."

Mandy reluctantly opened the box. Her jaw dropped.

"This is our way of saying we'd like you to come back to the Unicorn Club once and for all," I explained.

"Pretty gorgeous, huh?" Jessica gazed at the earrings.

I waited silently for Mandy to say something—that she was blown away, touched, or moved by the thoughtfulness of this gesture.

She opened her mouth, but nothing came out. She must have been at a loss for words.

"I remember feeling the same way when my dad surprised me with a diamond pendant," I said understandingly.

"Aren't you going to put them on?" Kimberly pressed. "They're *so* you."

"You know, my charm bracelet would look amazing with those," Jessica mused. "I'll let you borrow it if you want."

"But . . ." Mandy gulped and looked me straight in the eye. "I just . . . I can't accept these."

"What do you mean?" I replied. "They're a gift."

Mandy handed the box back to me.

"You've wanted them all year," I reminded her. "We've stared at them at the mall at least a million times. They're the exact pair, I'm positive. . . . "

"I know." Mandy looked down. "My mom put a pair on layaway. She's been saving to buy them for me for my birthday."

"But that's not for months," I argued. "Do you want to keep on wearing cheapo earrings that make your lobes all gross?"

"Lila!" Mandy responded.

"There's nothing to be embarrassed about. My ears can handle only precious metals, too. And don't worry about your mom," I said soothingly. "She can buy you something else. Wouldn't you rather have them now than later?"

Mandy got up from the booth. "No," she said.

"But wouldn't it be better for your mom to save the money?" I pointed out. "She could use it for groceries or something that you guys really need. Like a decent TV."

Mandy's face turned red. "It means a lot to my mom to give me those earrings."

"OK, OK," I relented. "Then you can exchange them for something else you like at The Gold Rush. I was actually planning to go back there this weekend. You should see this stuff they just got in from Italy. Too gorgeous for words."

"I've got to go," Mandy said quickly, glancing at the clock on the wall.

"You still have to finish your explosion," Ellen pointed out.

Mandy strapped on her backpack. "There's somewhere I have to be."

"I'm sure it can wait," I said.

"It's important. OK?" Mandy said forcefully.

"Mandy!" I called out as she rushed for the door. But she didn't turn around.

I sank in my seat and stared at the little velvet box sitting on the table. What had I done wrong?

"Good one, Lila," Kimberly said sarcastically.

"How was I supposed to know her mom is buying them for her?" I said. "I thought this would be the icing on the cake." I pursed my lips. "At least I tried."

Ellen looked down. "Mandy must be getting really attached to the Angels."

Jessica sighed. "I guess it's going to take a lot more than a pair of gold earrings to drag her away from them."

"We'll get her back," I told my friends confidently. "I'll think of something."

Four

I can't believe I kept Randall waiting an extra hour just so I could spend time with the Unicorns, I thought as I rushed toward the hospital. I felt so guilty, I wanted to scream. If I had been doing something useful or mandatory, it would have been fair, but hanging out with the Unicorns sometimes feels like a big waste. And what was the deal with Lila giving me an expensive pair of earrings? Was she trying to flaunt her fortune and rub in the fact that my mom has to work hard to make ends meet?

Waiting at the crosswalk, millions of negative thoughts about the Unicorns flitted through my mind. Sometimes I can't believe how snobby they can be. Putting down Lois Waller was so cruel! And all their talk about the uselessness of environmental reforms really bugged me, too. I'm sure Lila thinks that her dad could just pay her housekeeper to go up in a helicopter and clean up the damage to the ozone with a mildew remover.

The Unicorns don't see the big picture. Their biggest concerns are about what they're wearing, who's going out with whom, and when the next Johnny Buck movie is getting released. It's not that I can't see the fun in that kind of stuff, but when you compare it with what's really important—like a seven-year-old battling it out with cancer—it's pretty frivolous.

It's hard to believe that there was a time, not so long ago, when I thought the Unicorns and I shared so much in common. I mean, I know the Unicorns have been wanting me back in the group, but every time I get a taste of their cattiness, I don't want to be associated with them at all. Ever. If they really wanted me to reconsider their offer, they could do it by being nicer to each other and other people. But the Unicorns showed me their true colors back at Casey's. They're shallow and mean-spirited and they'll never be any other way. I guess the time has come for me to move on and form new friendships.

I wish I could say that in my heart I belonged with the Angels. They do share my values about accepting people for what's inside rather than out-side and doing what they can for those in need. But most of the memories I share with them are of stuff like cataloging books at the library and selling gra-nola cakes at school. That stuff *is* important, but I like to let loose every once in a while, be daring, wild, or silly. Every time I've suggested doing something exciting like bungee jumping or water-skiing, they have their standard excuses. Evie says she has to practice her violin, Elizabeth tells me she needs to study, Maria will quote some statistic about how many water-skiers are injured every year, and Mary will admit that crazy things like that just aren't for her. Well, as far as I'm concerned, life's too short to play it safe.

The truth is that I feel like I don't *have* anyone to have fun with anymore. There are over a thousand students at Sweet Valley Middle School, and I feel totally alone. I don't know who to call a real friend.

But who am I to complain? I asked myself as I reached the hospital steps. So what if I'm friendless? I still have my health and my family and my home. And if I feel alone in the world, just think of how Randall must be feeling.

When I came in the hospital room, Randall was in bed, drawing on a big piece of poster paper.

"Hey, stranger," I said.

His face lit up. "Mandy!"

"I'm sorry I'm a little late," I apologized, taking a seat at his bedside.

"Just don't let it happen again," he teased.

"Whatcha' got there?" I asked, peering at his drawing.

"It's me and you," he said, pointing to two stick figures. "It's after I'm better, see? I have hair and stuff."

"But you forgot to add your freckles," I said. I pulled my special drawing pencils out of my backpack and added little brown spots to his cartoonlike face.

We took turns adding details to our pictures. He drew little flowers in my hair and a string of colored beads around my neck. I gave him a purple baseball cap and a triple-scoop ice-cream cone. Finally, Randall took a black crayon and wrote BEST FRENDS in block letters above the drawing. He left out the "i" in friends, which somehow made it even sweeter to me.

"It's true. Right?" he asked, pointing at the heading.

I grinned. "Add *i* to friends before the *e*, and it's a deal."

Randall squeezed in the i and looked at me hopefully. "Can we shake on it?"

I extended my hand. "Best friends," I agreed.

"Forever," he added.

My eyes welled up with tears. I guess I was wrong when I said I was alone in the world. I did, after all, have someone who was a lot like me. I bet Randall would never make fun of fat girls or say no to the chance to bungee jump. I'm sure he wouldn't judge someone by the price of their shoes and he'd probably love to try waterskiing. And even though he was only seven, I think he knew what it was that made life really special—having a best friend to share it with.

"You look like you're gonna cry," Randall said suddenly. "What's wrong?"

"I, well . . . the picture. It . . ." I stammered.

"You're just like my mom. She cries about *every-*

thing," Randall said. "You shoulda' seen her when I drew *her* picture."

I wiped a tear away. "That's what girls do, I guess."

"Look. If you like the picture so much, you can have it," Randall said cheerfully.

"I love it, Randall. I'll hang it above my desk in my bedroom." I took a breath, trying to compose myself. "Now. Are you ready for that game of checkers?"

He looked at me seriously. "I need to ask you something first."

I cleared away the crayons and pencils. "Shoot."

"Were you really scared?" He clutched his sheet. "You know, when you had cancer?"

I looked at him sympathetically. Even though his prognosis was good, I knew exactly how he felt. Randall could see for himself that a lot of kids didn't make it. I was glad to be an example of one who had.

"I was scared, all right," I confessed. "I cried a lot."

"I bet you did," he teased.

I giggled. "You know, it's OK to cry. Just because you're a boy doesn't mean you have to be all big and macho."

"I know, but . . ." He took off his baseball cap. "Did you feel real dumb when your hair fell out?"

"Trust me, it's worse when you're a girl," I told him. "I mean, I knew it was worth it because the medicine that made it happen was also going to make me better. But I felt really insecure, too.

My mom went out and bought me a wig."

"How'd it look?"

I grimaced at the memory. "Like a bad perm or something. It had to have been the ugliest thing I've ever seen in my whole life. I think that's how she ended up with it. It was on sale, and I guess no one else wanted it. I looked like Little Orphan Annie."

Randall started laughing, and then snorting. When Randall finds something superfunny, his laughter becomes full of snorts. I nudged him playfully. "Who knows? Maybe it would look better on you, being that you're a natural redhead," I said. "You can borrow it if you want."

"That's OK, I'll stick to the cap," he decided.

"Anyway, I was really afraid to go back to school in a curly mop of frizz," I went on. "I thought I was going to get teased by everyone. Especially the boys. And then one day all my friends came over to my house. They had pitched in and bought me a gorgeous wig that looked just like my hair."

"Your friends did that for you?" He sounded impressed.

"Well, yeah," I said slowly. "That's what friends do. Right?"

Randall wrinkled his nose in disagreement. "I got a card from all the kids in my class and all these puzzles and stuff, but nothing that good."

"Well, they came by and visited almost every day at my house," I continued, thinking back. The Unicorns really had been there for me. Especially

Jessica. And that was even before I had become officially part of the Unicorn Club.

"They sound like the greatest friends in the whole wide world," he said admiringly.

I smiled softly. "Well, they . . . yeah . . . I mean . . ." I broke off with a shrug. Maybe they *were* the greatest friends once, but it seemed like everyone had changed since then. This year, the Unicorns had become more boy-crazy, more catty, and more self-consumed than ever. They probably considered being do-gooders a thing of the past—a trend that had come and gone. If I were stuck in the hospital again, would they bother to visit me at all? I wanted to believe that they would be there, but I just wasn't sure anymore.

Randall sat up in bed. "So can I meet them sometime? Maybe you could bring them with you tomorrow."

I felt my chest tighten. I know how the Unicorns feel about volunteering their "precious" time. They don't even show up at the day-care center much anymore. If I asked them to come, Lila would probably have some grand excuse about an appointment with her manicurist or something. And Kimberly would say she had to go shopping and make a dozen phone calls before she could even *think* about spending time in the cancer ward.

"I don't know about that, Randall," I said sadly, "but you can definitely count on me."

Five

"Maybe Mandy had to rush off for a conference with a teacher or something," Ellen suggested. "It was like one of those miscommunication things. She'll probably eat lunch with us in the Unicorner tomorrow and tell us all about it."

"You're reaching, Ellen," I said. "She obviously didn't want us to know where she was going."

We were still sitting in our booth at Casey's, trying to figure out why Mandy had left in such a huff. Everybody but Kimberly had let their ice cream melt. Hers had ended smack on the floor when she accidentally knocked it over during a dramatic reenactment of Mandy's exit.

"We might as well accept it. She probably went to hang out with the Angels," Kimberly guessed.

"But how could she pick them over us?" I shook

my head in disbelief. "It just doesn't make sense. That's like picking carnations over roses."

"Or carob over chocolate," Kimberly added.

"Or Randy Mason over Aaron Dallas," Jessica said dreamily.

"Or spaghetti over pasta," Ellen went along.

"Spaghetti *is* pasta, Ellen," I snapped.

Ellen wrinkled her forehead, processing this new dose of information. "So that's why spaghetti with meat sauce tastes exactly the same as pasta bolognese?"

I was too upset about Mandy to stop and tease Ellen for being so Ellen. "What's your read of the situation, Jessica?" I asked.

Jessica shook her head. "I just don't get it. Mandy used to be so into being a Unicorn."

Ellen leaned her elbows on the table and cupped her chin in her fist. "And we were so proud to have her in the club."

I noticed Elizabeth come through the door. "There's Elizabeth," I said, sitting up straight. "Hey, Elizabeth," I yelled, "over here."

Kimberly frowned. "Since when are you so excited to hang out with Elizabeth Wakefield? No offense, Jessica, but your sister *is* an Angel."

"Exactly," I whispered. "I think it's time we do a little research on Mandy and the Angels. You know, find out what the Angels have that we don't."

Elizabeth reluctantly walked over to our table. "Hi."

"Sit down," I offered, patting the spot next to me.

"Me?" she asked warily.

"Yes. You can even finish my fudge brownie explosion," I said, pushing the melted glop her way.

Elizabeth eyed the bowl skeptically. "That looks like soup."

"So it's a little melted," I said. "It still tastes the same."

"Thanks, but I'm just waiting for Maria and Evie," she told us, looking back toward the entrance. "Actually I said I'd save a booth, and—"

Jessica grabbed Elizabeth's hand and pulled her into the booth. "Just talk to us for a second, Lizzie."

"What's up?" She sounded concerned.

"Well, we wanted to congratulate you," Jessica replied.

Elizabeth leaned toward Jessica. "For what?" she asked.

"I guess you guys are winning so far," Jessica said, tucking a wisp of hair behind her ear.

"The Angels must be cooler than we think if Mandy would rather be in your club," Kimberly added.

"How on earth did you do it?" I asked curiously.

"I . . . I don't know what you're talking about," Elizabeth answered. "It doesn't look like Mandy's into being an Angel at all."

"It doesn't?" we all said in unison.

"We *wish* she would be. The bake sale today was the first time she's worked with us in weeks."

Elizabeth exhaled and fidgeted with the barrette in her hair. "Mandy's been so busy after school, we just assumed that she's leaning toward the Unicorns again."

"Well, that's a good sign!" Ellen yelped.

"True," I agreed slyly. "That means Mandy's still in limbo, not leaning toward either club."

"How weird, though. I mean, what do you think she's been up to?" Elizabeth asked.

I frowned. If Mandy wasn't hanging out with the Angels and she wasn't attending Unicorn meetings, either, where *had* she been?

When the final bell rang the next afternoon, the Mysterious Departures of Mandy were still driving me crazy. But I knew how to get to the bottom of the matter—I'd follow her. Once I found out her destination, I could feign my own interest in her new hobby, and—presto!—instant bonding.

Slipping on a pair of dark sunglasses, I followed Mandy as she exited the building.

Mandy walked briskly uptown. I stayed about fifty yards behind her, ducking behind mailboxes and telephone poles every time she waited at a crosswalk. Mandy abruptly turned the corner and headed toward Steps, a dance studio where lots of kids from Sweet Valley take classes. So that was it. Tap lessons. Or, knowing Mandy, probably modern dance. But why did she have to keep it such a big secret? I hung back, waiting for her to enter, but she passed right by the building.

I heaved a sigh. So much for my dance class theory.

Mandy whizzed through the shopping district, not even pausing to window-shop at any of our favorite spots. She turned the corner by the post office and leaned over for a second to tie her shoelace. Her pace slowed again when we neared the front of Valley View, the retirement home. Was Mandy a volunteer? She tilted her head and peered through the lobby window, but she never actually stopped. She just kept on walking. And walking. And walking. I'd have worn hiking boots if I'd known what I was in for.

We'd been en route for almost half an hour when Mandy turned up a pathway. I looked at the building she was moving toward, and my stomach dropped. She was entering the Sweet Valley Children's Hospital! Had her cancer come out of remission? Had her tumor spread? Was Mandy dying? Why would she hide something like this from us?

"Lookin' for someone?" a young nurse asked as she approached me.

"Yes!" I exclaimed breathlessly. I had sprinted up the hospital steps and rushed inside the building, urgent to find out what was going on with Mandy. She was nowhere in sight.

"Are you OK?" the nurse asked with a thick Texas accent as she got closer. The name tag on her white uniform read NURSE TALKINGTON.

My jaw was so tense, it was hard to talk. "I'm fine, but I . . . I . . . I need to know if a friend of mine is a patient here. I just saw her come in here, and—"

"You mean Mandy?" the nurse said loudly.

"Yes! Oh, no. Tell me. No, don't tell me. Oh, just tell me." I leaned against the wall and braced myself. I could feel my heart pounding.

"Tell you what?" she inquired.

"Is she sick?" I buried my face in my hands.

"Sick?" the nurse repeated. "Heck, no."

"No?" I slowly looked up at her.

"N-O," she spelled out with a friendly smile.

"Are you sure?" I asked cautiously.

"Absolutely positively."

I sighed with tremendous relief. "Oh thank goodness."

"I agree, because I don't know what we'd do without her. She's been volunteering here every day."

"Every day?" I repeated.

"Rain or shine. She's taken a real likin' to a boy named Randall Boyer."

I raised my eyebrows. So that was it. Mandy had fallen for a cancer patient. Suddenly, her distraction made perfect sense. I know I can get sidetracked when I have a boy on my mind. "Is he totally adorable or something?" I asked.

"Oh, yeah. A real cutie pie. Even though he's as bald as a bowling ball."

"Well, when you have really good facial structure and high cheekbones, you can easily pull off the hairless thing," I explained, recalling how hot Johnny Buck looked when he shaved it all off for *The Pirate*.

Nurse Talkington smiled. "Is that so?"

"What's he like?" I asked eagerly.

Nurse Talkington batted her eyelashes fondly. "He's sweet, silly, artistic, and he plays a mean game of checkers."

Not exactly the characteristics I look for in a guy, but Mandy's always had kooky taste.

"All the nurses are crazy for him," she added.

"A total charmer, huh?" I just hoped he wouldn't dump Mandy for a blond bimbo when he recovered. Stuff like that is not uncommon.

"In his own way," she agreed.

"So, wait, are they, like, in love?" I had to know for sure.

Nurse Talkington's eyes widened. *"In love?"* she repeated.

I shrugged. "Well, yeah." I didn't see why she was so weirded out. It sounded like a normal enough question to me.

She looked as though she was trying not to laugh. "Well, I wouldn't say they're in love, no. It would be pretty unlikely, since Randall's only seven."

I cleared my throat. "Seven?"

"Actually, the other day he told me he was almost seven and a half," she said.

I scratched my head. "You mean they're not a couple?"

She laughed. "It's like a big sister–little brother kind of a thing I s'pose."

I felt more confused than ever. Why would Mandy devote all her spare time to a little boy? "So what is she doing with him?" I asked. "I mean, why would she blow off everyone else in her life to hang with a sick kid?"

Nurse Talkington held up her hands. "I told you, hon, they have a good time together. Just wait till you meet the little fireball. Maybe then you'll understand."

I shrugged. "Whatever."

"Ya see, he's here all alone," the nurse went on. "His mother lives over six hours away."

I frowned. "Isn't there a hospital closer to home? Does he live in some remote mountain range or something?"

"Well, this is the very best oncology institute in all of California," she explained. "His mom can only visit on the weekends, so sweet li'l Mandy has taken it upon herself to be here for him."

"But why him?"

"I suppose the whole thing has struck a chord in her," she began. "She's been a great help to the family. Course she's the first to tell ya that the best situation would be to get Randall's mother down here permanently. But financially speaking, that's just not possible." Nurse Talkington shook her head sorrowfully. "The poor gal is broke enough as it is."

"Broke?" I slowly repeated.

Nurse Talkington put her hands on her hips. "With a capital *B*."

Did this mean that a little bit of money could solve the entire crisis?

"I know how badly Mandy wishes she could help in that regard," the nurse went on. "But she's doin' all she can. And we all know that money doesn't grow on trees."

"Oh, I don't know about that," I said, a smile growing on my face. "You'd be surprised."

"So what's the big fuss?" Kimberly demanded as I opened the front door for her, Jessica, and Ellen.

After my visit to the hospital I had called an emergency meeting at my house.

"Really, Lila, I was in the middle of unclogging my pores," Jessica complained. "That avocado-and-mayonnaise mask was just starting to feel tingly."

"Trust me, I'm not wasting your time," I assured them, leading the way into the living room. "I know how we can get Mandy back in the Unicorns."

"You do?" Jessica yelped.

"Really?" Ellen grasped her hands together hopefully.

I told them the whole story about Randall and his mom, pumping up the tragedy for a little added drama. "Can you imagine how terrible it would be, being all alone in a cold, stark hospital room? Crying yourself to sleep every night, not knowing if you would live to see eight candles on your birthday cake?" I said in conclusion.

"I don't believe it." Ellen shook her head. "Hospital rooms are cold? Can't they heat them?"

"That's not really the point, Ellen." I rolled my eyes.

"What *is* the point? What does this have to do with Mandy rejoining the Unicorns?" Kimberly demanded.

"Everything," I replied. "If we can fix things for Randall and his mom, Mandy will see how great we are. She'll be so touched that she'll instantly rejoin the club."

"But we don't even know him," Ellen pointed out.

"Who cares," I said impatiently. "We're just going to do it to make Mandy happy. Don't you want her back?"

"Of course we do," Kimberly agreed. "But I still don't see what we can possibly do."

"Maybe we can find a cure for his cancer," Ellen suggested.

I couldn't help grinning. You've got to admire Ellen's imaginative spirit. "That's an interesting thought, Dr. Riteman, but I have a more *realistic* idea. The way I look at it is that there's nothing that money can't buy. Right?"

"You can't buy your health back," Jessica said.

"I know that, Jessica," I snapped. "What I mean is that if we gave Randall's mom a bunch of money, she could afford to take a leave of absence from her job and stay in the hotel down the street from the hospital. That way she could see Randall every day."

"But we don't have that kind of cash!" Kimberly remarked.

"Lila does," Jessica said, turning toward me.

I smiled at her appreciatively. Finally, someone was on my wavelength.

"So is it a done deal?" Jessica asked.

"Not exactly." I had considered taking a withdrawal from my dad's funds, but ultimately had decided against it. "I do have personal access to my dad's bank account, but he expects me to use it with discretion."

"So how are we supposed to pay for the hotel and everything?" Kimberly asked.

"Our dues fund is running pretty low," Ellen pointed out.

"You guys are overlooking the obvious." I put my hands on my hips. "I don't just stand to inherit my dad's fortune; I've also inherited his money-making genes."

"You want to *raise* the money?" Jessica complained. "That's a terrible idea."

"That'll take work," Kimberly added with a grimace.

"Not if we're really crafty," I explained. "Tap into the marketplace; think about what's in demand these days."

"That'll take forever," Kimberly noted.

"And Rome wasn't built in a day." I crossed my

arms over my chest. "Are you guys in or not?"

"Oh, why not," Jessica consented. "Let's give it a try."

"Mandy's worth it," Ellen declared.

"So how do you suggest we raise this small fortune?" Kimberly asked.

"How about a car wash?" Jessica suggested. "No overhead as far as supplies."

"And get all dirty and wet?" I replied. "Please, that's too much hard work."

"You know, there's big money in tutoring," Ellen told us.

"How would you know?" Kimberly asked.

"Because I have a math tutor twice a week now. I cannot *believe* how much my mom pays her."

Kimberly sighed. "And how could you expect to *be* a tutor if you *have* a tutor?"

"I don't know," Ellen replied defensively. "We could post signs at the elementary school. I can easily handle anything up to fourth-grade math."

"Forget it," Kimberly responded. "None of us are qualified, anyway." She smoothed her hair behind her ears. "Although I did get an *A* minus on my algebra quiz."

I cleared my throat to get everyone's attention. "Here's the way I see it," I began. "Not everybody needs their car washed. Not everybody needs a math tutor. But *everybody* needs cookies."

Ellen licked her lips. "A bake sale?"

"It's a sure thing," I said confidently.

"We could set up outside the supermarket. Nab

the customers before they go for the store-bought kind," Jessica suggested.

"I have a better idea," I said. "We'll go door-to-door selling cookies in my neighborhood. When all these rich people hear that we're trying to raise money for a poor sick boy, how can they say no? It would be an injustice."

"A disgrace!" Jessica said dramatically.

Kimberly banged her fists on the couch. "An appalling act of wrongdoing."

I smiled. "Then it's settled. Bring your aprons to school. We'll bake tomorrow," I announced.

Six

"Snickerdoodles," Ellen shouted out excitedly. "That's what we should make."

I looked up from the different boxes of sugar I'd set on the counter. "*What* are snickerdoodles?" I asked Ellen.

Ellen sat up straight on her stool. "You mean you don't know? I know something that you don't?"

Ellen was obviously taking incredible pleasure in being privy to knowledge that had somehow passed me by, because she started dancing around the room.

"No, for some strange reason, I have no idea what snickerdoodles are," I said, watching Ellen spin around.

"Then I'm not telling," she teased, skipping.

I tossed my hair over my shoulders. "Oh, well, then I guess we can't make them."

"They're sugar cookies," Kimberly filled in.

"Then why don't you just call them that?" I asked.

"Makes them sound more interesting," Ellen replied, trotting back over to the stool.

It was Thursday, and as planned the Unicorns had gathered in my kitchen. Aprons on, hair pulled back, we were ready to bake as soon as we agreed on what type of cookies to make. But as our history shows, it's never easy for the four of us to make a decision. Even in matters as trivial as baking.

For someone who's into cooking, our kitchen is a dream. There's a huge wooden block in the middle used for prepping food. Above it hang copper pots and pans in every shape and size. The pantry holds as much food as in a mini-supermarket. The tiles are all imported from Italy. Each one is hand painted with a different fruit or vegetable. And the best part about it is that once you've made a mess, Mrs. Pervis will come in and clean up after you. Of course we wouldn't exactly *have* anything to clean if we couldn't decide what kind of cookies to make.

"Well, we're not making your doodlydoos or whatever they're called. We're dealing with an upscale clientele," I explained. "We need to make something that they're going to be interested in actually buying."

Jessica scratched her head. "How about spice cookies?"

"Well, we want to be able to enjoy the batter, too," I said.

Ellen pushed herself up on the counter. "Good point."

"Almond cookies?" Kimberly blurted out. "What do you think?"

"A lot of people don't like nuts," I answered.

"I guess that would eliminate peanut butter cookies." Ellen sighed.

"And walnut squares," Kimberly added.

"How about chocolate fudge drops?" Jessica licked her lips.

"Too rich," I replied.

"Butter cookies?" Kimberly offered.

"Too bland," I answered.

"I'm telling you, snickerdoodles are the way to go," Ellen insisted.

I groaned. "Where's Jean Luc when you really need him?"

"Don't you remember?" Ellen remarked. "He's on vacation."

I shook my head. "I know that, Ellen."

Jessica pointed to the shelf full of cookbooks. "But maybe we could use one of his recipes."

I nodded and slipped out a book called *Delicious Desserts*. I scanned the index's alphabetical listing of cookies: amaretto cake, apple dumplings, bear claws, berry crumbles, candied apples . . . "Duh," I said as my eyes caught the next entry. "We're overlooking the obvious. The old standard."

"Chocolate chip cookies," Jessica and Kimberly sang in unison.

"Is it a unanimous decision?" I looked to Ellen for her approval.

"Is there such a thing as a presidential veto in a situation like this?" she asked.

I put my hands on my hips. "Get over it, Ellen."

"Really. That's abusing your power," Kimberly scoffed.

"I'm just kidding!" Ellen giggled. "Chocolate chip cookies sound awesome."

"Good. Then let's get to work." I began rattling off the list of ingredients to my helpers. "Baking soda, flour, brown sugar . . ."

Once everything was in front of me, I turned back to the directions. "What do you guys think? Should we triple or quadruple the batch?"

Jessica adjusted her apron. "What's the worst thing that happens? We have leftovers to take home."

Kimberly removed the measuring cup from the cupboard and handed it to me. "And wouldn't that be a drag," she joked.

"Quadruple it," I agreed. "Let's see, quadrupling eggs are easy," I said, cracking a few into the bowl. "But what's one and three fourths of a cup times four? I think I need a calculator."

"Eight," Kimberly replied.

"You sure?" I asked, pouring flour into the cup.

"Didn't I mention my *A* minus in math?" Kimberly bragged.

"Once or twice," I said, dumping eight cups of flour into the bowl along with the eggs and vanilla.

"I mean seven!" Kimberly shouted out.

I glared at Kimberly. "Good one, Kimberly."

Ellen examined the batter like a scientist. "You know, sometimes the best things are discovered by accident. You may have revolutionized this recipe. Remember how yummy those pancakes were that I put orange juice in?"

"I thought they made you sick," Jessica recalled.

"But you guys loved them," she reminded us.

"True. And what harm could a little extra flour be?" I decided. "I suppose we should just add some extra sugar to even it out."

"And some extra chocolate chips," Ellen added.

"Perfection," I said, after taking a bite of cookie batter from the wooden spoon.

Jessica licked some dough off her pointer finger. "Out of this world," she agreed.

Ellen took a bite and squinted her eyes, thinking. She clicked her tongue against the roof of her mouth, then dug in for a little more.

"This is a batter sampling, not a wine tasting, Ellen. What do you think?" I pressed.

"Scrumdidilyuptuous," Ellen said finally. "I think the extra ingredients give it a nice thick texture, and the nutmeg I put in by mistake is totally drowned out by the richness of the chocolate chips."

Kimberly used the wooden spoon to dig out a clump. "You're right. The finished product will be a taste of heaven."

We each took a cookie sheet and spooned out little blobs of dough. Finally the cookies were ready to hit the oven. I put on my mitts and carefully slid them into their places.

"You guys want to check out *Miami Madness* while they're baking?" I offered as I set the timer for twelve minutes.

Jessica's eyes lit up. "The Johnny Buck movie?"

"It's out on video already?" Kimberly exclaimed.

"Yes. We can watch the first ten minutes or so," I said, taking the timer along.

"Call the fire department!" Ellen squealed.

"Open the windows!" I yelled, running through the smoke-filled kitchen.

Jessica, Kimberly, and Ellen rushed in after me.

"I can't find them," Ellen shouted, hidden in a cloud of smoke. "Whoops, that's the fridge. Whoa . . ."

"Ouch!" Kimberly hollered. "That's me."

I fumbled for the oven and turned the heat off. I switched on the oven light, and we all stared in at the trays. Our first batch of cookies were history—burnt beyond recognition.

"I guess it was a mistake to stay glued to the surfing scene after the buzzer rang," Ellen said as she coughed from a dose of smoke inhalation.

"I know. But it's just so hard to tear yourself away from Johnny Buck in a bathing suit," I sighed. "Now let's try this again."

"Mega disaster," Jessica said, fanning the smoke with her hand.

"What a waste," Ellen said, examining the blackened blobs that accounted for our second unsuccessful round of chocolate chip cookies.

I turned to Jessica. "Why'd you have to talk us into catching some rays by the pool?" I scolded.

"It's such a gorgeous day," Jessica retorted. "And with our rosy cheeks, we'll make better cookie sellers."

"We don't *have* any cookies to sell," I pointed out.

Kimberly let out a frustrated sigh. "I give up."

"We can't give up," I pleaded. "This is the way to get Mandy back."

"Well, I don't have all day to hang around making burnt cookies," Kimberly said.

"Me either," Jessica agreed.

"Look. I'll just send the chauffeur out to buy us some cookies," I offered. "He doesn't have much to do with my dad gone."

"Forget it. Our profits will be way lower if we have to put money in to buy the cookies," Kimberly complained.

"I don't have any money, anyway," Jessica said glumly. "I'm already two allowances in debt to Elizabeth."

"Don't worry. I'll pay," I told them.

"Well, if you're paying, what are we waiting for?" Jessica grinned.

"We should get that soft kind that seems homemade," Ellen recommended. "Our customers will never know the difference."

I hit the intercom button that connects me with

Charles's room. "Charles," I requested, "could I see you for a minute?"

". . . and this sweet little boy is so sick. Even a small purchase will make a huge impact in his life," I said to the woman in skintight spandex standing in her doorway. She held a fluffy white poodle in her arms.

It was our fourth door-to-door visit, and I had gotten the sob story down to a two-minute spiel. Ellen held out the tray of cookies on a hand-painted platter, which I thought added to their illusion of being homemade. Jessica and Kimberly had gone off to the other side of the street together. We figured that splitting up would allow us to hit more homes in the same amount of time.

The woman fluffed her bleached-blond hair. "I'm really trying to watch my weight. I don't do well with temptations."

I considered running home for the sugar-free granola cakes in the freezer.

"But it's a good way to develop willpower," Ellen pointed out.

I cleared my throat. "Look. Maybe you didn't hear me clearly. This boy has the C word. Cancer. How will you live with yourself if you don't help?"

Ellen sniffled. "How?"

"I do wish I could do something," she said. "How about a donation?"

"That'd be fabulous," I agreed.

"Let me grab my purse." She put down her poodle.

As she ran down the hallway, Ellen helped herself to a cookie.

"You're eating all the inventory!" I scolded.

"This is hard work, Lila. This tray weighs a ton." She took a big bite. "I need the energy to keep going."

"It is sort of draining," I admitted, helping myself to one.

The woman returned with a check. "Here you go, girls."

I graciously took the check from her, not looking at the amount. I didn't want to seem greedy in front of her.

Once I had thanked her and she had closed the door, I anxiously stared down at her scribble. "A dollar fifty? She gave us a check for a dollar and fifty cents."

Ellen looked over my shoulder at the pink polka-dot check. "That was all she could spare? How could she be so stingy? There were diamonds on her dog's collar!"

I shrugged with disappointment and slipped the check in my pocket. "Let's just hope that Jessica and Kimberly are having better luck."

"These people are misers," Jessica complained. "They're probably big fans of Scrooge."

When Ellen and I met up with Jessica and Kimberly in the middle of the street, we found that they'd encountered similarly stingy cookie customers. Jessica, who has an incredible flair as a salesperson, hadn't been able to weasel more than four dollars out of anyone.

Kimberly tallied up our money as we glumly walked back to my house.

"Well," Kimberly announced regretfully. "We've got a grand total of . . . twelve dollars and seventy-five cents."

"That won't even pay for a night in a hotel," I said sadly.

"This is your fault, Lila. You're the one who said your neighbors are big spenders," Jessica reminded me. "We could have done better on my street."

"Maybe they've spent so much on their houses and stuff that they don't have a lot of cash to spare," Ellen suggested.

"Relax, OK? We'll just have to find a more generous customer," I decided.

"Have anyone in mind?" Kimberly asked.

I wiggled my eyebrows mischievously. "Oh, yeah."

"Daddy?" I said sweetly into the phone.

"I'm in the middle of a critical meeting, honey. What's the emergency?" my father said quickly. "You're OK, aren't you?"

I had talked my dad's secretary into tracking down my dad at his meeting in New York.

"Well, I'm alive," I said. "But my heart? It's breaking."

"Honey, look, as long as everything is OK, I've really got to get back inside. We're talking numbers. I can't keep the investors waiting."

I knew if I drew this out as long as possible, my dad would be frantic to get off the phone. So frantic, he'd agree to *anything*. "It's a terribly, horribly tragic story. I'll just start at the very beginning. This boy's got cancer, and we're trying to—"

"Make it quick, Lila," he interrupted. "What can I do?"

"Buy some cookies from the Unicorns."

"Put me down for as many boxes as you want," he agreed. "I'll call you later, honey."

"Bye, Daddy." I hung up with a flourish.

"Well," Jessica asked eagerly. "What'd he say?"

My dad's offer of "as many boxes as you want" gave me a lot of leeway. "He's in for a thousand boxes," I announced.

Ellen gasped. "A thousand?"

I smiled triumphantly. "Only let's not actually buy the cookies, 'cause he'd just have to pay for those, too."

"Mandy is going to be so psyched!" Kimberly exclaimed.

It was Friday afternoon, and the Unicorns had piled into my dad's limo. We were en route to the hospital to present Mandy with a fat envelope of cash.

"What would you say if someone gave you three thousand eleven dollars and seventy-five cents?" Ellen asked.

We had decided that three dollars per box was a reasonable amount to charge my dad and had tallied in the money we'd earned by going door-to-door.

"I'd faint," Jessica answered matter-of-factly.

"I just hope it's enough," I said. "When you think about it, it might not make up for all her lost wages. I mean three thousand dollars isn't exactly enough to change a person's life."

"It would change mine," Ellen declared. "I'd sign up for horseback-riding lessons, buy a new wardrobe at the Valley Mall, and take all you guys for a vacation in Hawaii. Or would you rather go somewhere that's tropical in Mexico, or—"

"Anyway," Jessica butted in, "maybe she won't take a leave of absence from her job, but she'll be able to spend a little more time with Wendall."

"Randall," I corrected her. "You know, I never even stopped to think how much all those medical expenses are costing them. They may not have health insurance. Maybe we should go back to the bank. I could withdraw a little more."

"Forget it, Lila," Kimberly said forcefully. "It's the thought that counts."

But a thought is one thing. Really impacting someone's life is something else. I just wished there was something else I could do to make a difference. A real difference. A way to show Mandy how extraordinary the Unicorns can be.

I peered out the window as we drove through the quaint neighborhood that borders the hospital.

I saw girls playing hopscotch on the sidewalk and a cluster of kids gathered around an ice cream truck. Suddenly my eye caught a FOR SALE sign planted in the lawn of a little house. A banner ran across the sign that read OPEN HOUSE.

"Stop!" I shouted.

"Certainly, Miss Lila." Charles, who is used to my abrupt instructions, screeched to a halt in front of the house.

"What are you doing, trying to give us whiplash?" Kimberly hollered, massaging her neck.

"What's going on?" Jessica asked.

"Chill out," I demanded, my eyes still fixed on the little house. It was one story, surrounded by a charming white picket fence. The lawn was perfectly manicured, and there were flower boxes attached to the windows.

"Why are we stopping here?" Kimberly demanded.

"It's pretty, isn't it?" I said.

"What?" Ellen asked.

"The house. I'd better go check it on the inside before I get too excited. Why don't you guys relax for a few minutes. Charles? Could you pop in a Johnny Buck CD for my friends?" I jumped out of the car.

"Lila! What's going on?" Jessica yelled after me.

I strolled down the path that led to the front door of the house, ignoring my friends. "I'm going to make a real difference," I said to myself.

*   *   *

"I know it's nothing to brag about, but this is really an up-and-coming neighborhood. Did you see all those little kids playing in the street? It was so adorable." I leaned back in my seat. "And it'll be so much more comfortable than a hotel. Plus it has the benefit of being around the corner from the hospital. And apparently there's room to build a pool in the backyard."

"That's worth a lot more than a thousand boxes of cookies," Jessica pointed out.

"Big deal. One thousand boxes, one hundred thousand boxes. The difference is inconsequential to my dad. Besides," I added, perking up in my seat, "can you imagine how impressed Mandy will be?"

Seven

"Maybe we could invent a super-fast jet that could take my mom back and forth every night." Randall picked up a silver crayon.

I was sitting in a metal chair nudged up against his hospital bed. I'd rushed to the hospital after school and had been drawing pictures with him all afternoon.

"That way she'd be able to tuck me in at night, eat breakfast with me in the morning, and she could still be at her job by nine," Randall went on. "It could land on the roof of her office building."

I examined the drawing. "It could be like a house on the inside. Like a motor home with wings. So she'll be comfortable during the flight."

"Maybe there could be a pool on the wings," he suggested fervently. "She loves swimming."

"And there'd definitely be a game room with a

pinball machine, a trampoline, and a Ping-Pong table," I added, tearing off a fresh sheet of construction paper. "For when you went in it. We'd better add all this stuff to the blueprints."

"Think we could have it done by Tuesday?" he asked hopefully.

Tuesday was the day Randall had been dreading for weeks. It was the day he went in for surgery. His mom had done everything she could, but her heartless boss had maintained his position: one more day off for Randall would lead to her immediate dismissal. The hospital staff even had tried to shift the operation to Saturday, when she'd be around, but it was impossible. The doctor's schedule was too hectic. And putting the surgery off even one additional week would be potentially dangerous for Randall.

"If there was anything in the world that I could wish for, I'd hire the most brilliant engineers in Sweet Valley, have the jet manufactured, and even get my pilot's license so I could personally fly your mom down. But . . ." I looked down.

He leaned forward. "But what?"

I shook my head sadly. "But it's impossible."

"I know that." He brushed his hand over the drawing. "It's still fun to think about it, though."

"It sure is," I agreed.

"I just wish she could be here when I go in for the surgery," he said softly.

"She would if she could," I told him.

"But you'll be here, Mandy, won't you?"

I nodded. "You don't have to wish for that. Of course I will. And so will Nurse Talkington. And Dr. Baron is a really good guy. He's a world-renowned pediatric surgeon."

"What's that mean?" he asked.

"That he's super talented," I answered. "He's been around for a really long time and he's helped a lot of people with cancer get better. You know, he's the one who operated on me."

"Looks like he did a pretty cool job, too." Randall readjusted himself under the covers and yawned.

"You look tired," I said.

Randall opened his eyes widely, trying to look alert. "No. I'm fine. Let's play tic-tac-toe."

I smiled gently. "It's OK if you're tired." I pulled the covers up around him.

He frowned. "But I don't want you to go yet. It's still early." He pointed at the wall clock, which read three forty-five.

I clicked my tongue against the roof of my mouth, thinking. "I'll tell you what. You can take a nap. I'll sit in the hall and catch up on my homework. I'll be back in an hour. And then we can play a game and hang around together until visiting hours are over."

"Sounds like a good idea." His eyes shut slowly.

I pulled off his baseball cap, kissed his cheek, and watched Randall drift off to sleep.

*   *   *

I paced the corridor outside Randall's room, my stomach in knots. Somehow I just couldn't concentrate on my homework. Randall's jet plane drawings were getting to me—it killed me that he had to go in for surgery with his mom so far away. I had to take action.

"Nurse Talkington?" I asked, approaching the nurses' station.

"Hey, Dandy Mandy. What's up, doll?" She pushed some papers aside.

I leaned up against the counter and exhaled. "It's Randall," I said. "Isn't there any way his surgery could be bumped up to the weekend? When his mother's here?"

"I see what you're saying, Mandy, but the doc's schedule's full," she explained.

"But do you realize how afraid he is?" I asked. "Couldn't I talk to Dr. Baron? He was so wonderfully nice to me when I was sick, I . . . I just know if he understood what was going on with Randall he could make an exception."

Nurse Talkington tucked a pencil behind her ear. "Already took it upon myself to talk to the old guy. He can't do it. We all know it's not the ideal circumstances, but it'll be OK. Randall's a fighter."

"But he's only seven," I reminded her.

She came out from behind the nurses' station and put her arm around me. "You've done so much for Randall, sweetie pie. But sometimes a situation isn't in your control. He's got the best care, and the best nurse." She patted her chest proudly. "And he's got the greatest pal. You've already made a world of difference for his recovery."

"I hope so."

Nurse Talkington walked me back to the waiting area outside Randall's room. I guess she was right. They weren't the ideal circumstances, but Randall would get through it. I had done everything I could.

"This way!" I heard a raspy voice shout out as I sat outside Randall's room, trying to study my vocabulary words for English.

"Stop checking out the orderlies, Jessica! Let's move it."

Jessica?

"I'm right behind you, Lila. Chill."

Lila?

I looked down the corridor and found the faces that matched the names: Jessica, Lila, Kimberly, and Ellen were running my way. What were they doing here?

"Mandy!" Kimberly yelled eagerly as she caught my eye. "There she is," she informed the troop behind her as she ran toward me.

"Mandy!" Lila's face lit up.

"Cool nail polish," Jessica said, stopping in front of me.

I looked down at my multicolored fingernails, then back at the Unicorns, who had clustered around. "Wh-what are you guys doing here?" I'd hardly talked to them since the incident at Casey's, and I had kept my visits to Randall a secret.

"We came to see you," Ellen explained.

"But how'd you . . . why'd you . . . ?"

"Look, Mandy, we know all about sweet little Kendall," Jessica told me.

Lila glared at Jessica. "She *means* Randall."

"But, how?" I asked, completely confused.

"It doesn't matter how. Let's just say that we've solved all your problems," Lila boasted.

"You guys aren't making any sense at all," I told them.

"We know how much Randall means to you. We know how much you wish his mom could be here for him," Lila said passionately.

I widened my eyes. "But how'd you know? I never told anyone, I . . ."

"I did a little research, OK?" Lila explained, flipping her hair to the side. "I just *had* to know what was so important to you that you'd pass up the opportunity to hang out with us."

"We miss you, Mandy," Ellen said sincerely.

"And if Kendall, uh, Randall's important to you, then he's important to us, too," Jessica added.

"Really?" I asked tentatively.

"And truly," Kimberly said.

"I . . . I don't know what to say." Maybe I had been wrong to keep Randall a secret from the Unicorns. Maybe they really could understand after all.

"Your worries are over." Lila smiled proudly.

"They are?" I asked.

She nodded. "From now on, Randall's mom will be able to be here every single day. We bought her this adorable house right around the corner. Actually, I bought it, but you can consider it a gift from the Unicorns."

"It is, in spirit," Kimberly added, smiling angelically.

"Wh-what?" I asked, feeling a little dizzy.

"What's Randall's mom's name, by the way? I'll need to know that for the papers and stuff," Lila said.

"I don't think I'm following you," I said breathlessly. "I thought you just said you bought Randall's mom a house."

"You're hearing 20/20," Ellen assured me.

"That's how you measure vision, dummy," Kimberly told her, then turned to me. "In other words, Mandy, you heard her correctly. Lila bought Randall's mom a house. She just closed the deal."

I shook my head and leaned forward. "No way," I replied flatly.

Lila smiled triumphantly. "The address is 1642 Kearsarge Court. Of course it's not huge, but it's very homey. I'll have a key for her by tomorrow. I suppose we'll have to arrange for a moving van and all that. I hope her furniture matches the rustic feel of the house. If it doesn't, I might be able to arrange to have a few pieces sent over from our storage space."

My heart was racing. I didn't even care about

how Lila had found out about Randall anymore. Obviously, Lila thought she had discovered a simple solution. A solution that only money could buy. "You . . . you think you can just go throwing your dad's fortune around?"

"Sure." Lila beamed. "Isn't it *wonderful* that I'm in a position to help the less fortunate?"

I felt a hot flash overwhelm my body.

"You know, the sickly?" Lila continued. "The poor, downtrodden—"

"A new house isn't going to make Randall get better!" I interrupted angrily.

Lila looked a little taken aback. "Well, it's not going to hurt, either."

"But you can't go around buying people houses," I exclaimed.

Lila frowned slightly. "Of course I can. I mean, I did."

I clenched my fists. "But Randall's mom, whose name by the way is Christine Boyer, could never accept a house from a bunch of thirteen-year-olds."

"Why not?" Lila asked, totally stupefied.

"Because it's ridiculous and patronizing, and she already has a place to live," I replied, my voice rising. "In *northern* California."

Lila cleared her throat. "Well, she'll have a second home then. Very cosmopolitan."

Jessica clutched Lila's arm. "I think Mandy's saying no to the house, Lila!" she hissed.

Lila put her hands on her hips. "Oh, come *on*. What kind of a dummy would say no to this opportunity?

We're just making a charitable contribution."

"Well, it's not accepted," I told her feverishly. "Just return the house, or cancel the deal, or whatever you have to do."

Lila exhaled. "What is this deal with you not accepting gifts, Mandy? I mean, you should be touched by how much the Unicorns care about you. Can't you see that we just want you to be happy?"

"Wait a second," I said slowly. "You want *me* to be happy?"

"Yeah, we thought it'd make your day when Lila gave you those earrings at Casey's," Ellen began.

The earrings? I thought.

Suddenly something clicked. Lila had known for months how much I wanted the gold daisy studs. And now she was trying to buy me back into the club. Why hadn't this occurred to me sooner?

"And, well, when that wasn't enough, Lila decided we should really go out on a limb and do something to blow your mind," Ellen rambled.

I felt my face heat up as all the pieces fit into place. "So this has nothing to do with Randall." My voice was shaking. "You guys couldn't care less about what happens to him. This is some weird conniving way to get me back into the club!"

Lila put her hands on her hips. "So what if it is? We're just showing you that we'd do anything for you. I mean, do you think the Angels would go as far as buying you a house?"

"Of course they wouldn't!" I shouted. "Nobody with a normal sense of values would even consider it."

"But who ever wanted to be normal? We're the Unicorns. We're the best friends you could ever have," Lila pressed.

I stared at her, feeling my eyes fill with tears. "No, you're not. Just because you're rich doesn't mean you're nice people or good friends. So just leave me and Randall and his mom alone," I said hotly. "Maybe there are a lot of things that your daddy can buy you, Lila, but I'm not one of them!"

Lila reached for my arm. "Mandy, don't be—"

"Don't even try," I told her, jerking my arm away. "I don't want to have anything to do with you. You're shallow and spoiled and totally clueless!"

The color drained from Lila's face. Her mouth dropped open, but words didn't come out.

Kimberly shifted her feet uncomfortably. "Uh. Well . . ."

Jessica nervously tugged on Lila's sleeve. "Lila? Uh . . . maybe we should go."

"The exit's that way," I shouted, pointing down the corridor with my trembling hand.

Lila bowed her head and followed the others out of the building. I had obviously made my point. And if there ever had been any lingering doubt about it, there wasn't now—I had severed my ties with the Unicorn Club for good.

*   *   *

"Mandy? If you're not going to eat your hamburger, I'll take it," my little brother, Archie, said.

The events at the hospital had left me in a state of shock. After what happened with the Unicorns, I could hardly speak, let alone eat dinner. A strategically placed vase of fresh flowers had been hiding my untouched plate of food from my mother's view. Until Archie had blown my cover, anyway.

I gave Archie a "thanks a lot" glare.

"Uh-oh," my mom said. "I know what it means when Mandy isn't eating."

"It means I'm not very hungry," I told her. The last thing I wanted to do was tell my mother about what was going on with the Unicorn Club. Talking about it would only upset me more.

My mom peered over the flowers and looked at my plate. "Honey, a mother's intuition is always right. What's on your mind?"

I had so much pent-up anger that I felt totally on edge. Even thinking about what Lila had tried to do made me want to scream. "Nothing," I snapped. "Could you just leave me alone?"

"Mandy!" my mother scolded.

I stared down at my plate, feeling a little guilty. "I'm sorry. I—I didn't mean to sound so angry."

"If you've got something that's bothering you, Mandy, you should talk about it," my older sister, Cecilia, said. "That's what I do," she added, living up to my nickname for her, Saint Cecilia.

If there were an award for The Model Child of

America, my sister would be the recipient. She's neat, kind, and caring. She's also made the honor roll at Sweet Valley High School every semester since ninth grade. Next to her, I feel like some kind of lowly creature.

"Nothing ever bothers you, Cecilia. How would you know?" I asked her.

"That's not true," Cecilia argued.

I sighed. "Can we just change the subject? Like let's plan the menu for the anniversary party. It's just a couple of days away. We'd better get to it." My mom was throwing a fiftieth anniversary dinner party for my great-aunt and uncle.

"We already chose the menu," Cecilia replied. "Leg of lamb and vichyssoise."

"Oh," I said with disappointment as I began searching for another distracting topic.

"Mandy?" my mom asked sympathetically. "Are you upset about Randall?"

I thought about just saying yes and putting an end to the question-and-answer session. But it seemed unfair to use him as a scapegoat. "No. No more than usual, anyway," I admitted.

"Is he doing all right?" she pressed.

"Well, he's a little scared about his surgery, but I . . . I think he'll be fine." I turned to Cecilia. "Why don't you tell us all about that term paper you've been researching?"

My mom reached over and touched my arm. "Does this bad mood have anything to do with the fact that you haven't been wearing purple to school?"

I guess there's something to be said for a mother's intuition. I cringed.

"And that your friends haven't been hanging around here lately?" Cecilia added. "Not that I mind."

Cecilia's never been a big fan of the Unicorn Club. In her opinion they're "spoiled, pretentious, and lacking in substance." Funny that it's taken me so long to see her point.

"What friends?" I asked.

My mom's eyes twinkled. "That would be Kimberly, Lila—"

"Jessica," Archie added. Archie, like most boys in the world, has a special place in his heart for Jessica.

". . . and Ellen," my mom continued.

I cleared my throat. "Didn't you hear me? They're *not* my friends anymore. My membership with the Unicorns is officially over."

Archie sank in his seat. "You quit? But . . . I'll never be able to see her again."

"It's no loss," I replied.

"What happened?" my mom asked with concern.

"I'd rather not get into the details," I replied, pushing my salad around my plate with my fork. "Let's just say that the Unicorns have turned into a bunch of superficial snobs."

"I could have told you that," Cecilia responded.

"How disappointing," my mom said. "But at least this makes your decision about which club to choose a lot easier. I do think the Angels are a great group of girls."

While having a concerned mother can be a blessing, at times like this it feels like a curse. I wanted to keep all this to myself, crawl into a cave, and never face the fact that I had been let down by the group I had once called my best friends.

"I guess Elizabeth Wakefield is *almost* as good as Jessica," Archie decided.

I set down my fork and rested my head in my hands. It was no use keeping my feelings a secret from my family—they were going to pry them out of me one way or another. "I don't want to be an Angel, either. I know they're nice and I like to hang around them at school and stuff, but when it comes down to it, I don't feel like I fit in with them, either."

"I guess you're more independent than I thought," Cecilia said, sounding impressed.

"No. I'm not." I felt my throat swelling from emotion. "I . . . I'd love to be in a club again. I love the idea of having a close-knit group who does stuff together and leans on each other for support and everything. I, I . . ." Tears started to pour from my eyes, as I remembered how much the Unicorns used to mean to me.

"Sweetheart, it'll be OK." My mom stood up and rushed to my side.

"No, it won't. The only friend I have anymore is Randall." I wept harder. "And when he goes home, I'll have no one."

"So you can concentrate more on your school-work for once," Cecilia said optimistically. "You can meet me in the library after school tomorrow if you want."

I know she was only trying to make me feel better, but the thought of becoming a friendless bookworm, who spent all her free time in the library with her saintly sister, only made me feel worse. "Thanks, but no thanks," I said as I rushed away from the table.

Eight

Conniving? Clueless? Shallow? How could Mandy have said those things to me? I tried to shut out the words, but somehow they kept repeating themselves in my mind, all weekend long, as I did nothing but lie in bed and take long soaks in the tub. My friends tried to lure me out with talk of a shopping spree at the mall, but I couldn't motivate myself to join them. I had too much thinking to do.

I had always respected everything that Mandy said. I had always valued her opinion. I had always appreciated her honesty.

Which is why, I suppose, I couldn't help but wonder if I really *had* done something wrong. Something that was conniving, clueless, and shallow.

Maybe there are a lot of things that your daddy can buy you, Lila, I heard Mandy say, *but I'm not one of them!*

Was she right? I wondered as I sank into my down pillows. I wanted to believe she'd read me all wrong, but how could I? I was trying to buy her back into the Unicorn Club. And instead of bringing her closer, it had pushed her farther away.

I had always seen my dad's bank account as an answer to my problems. But where had all that money gotten me? It was good for the mansion and the clothes and the meals in fancy restaurants. But wouldn't I turn it all in in a split second for a really close, happy family? For a mother who told me all about her experiences as a teenager? A father who was there for me and would help me with my homework? Siblings who I could goof off with and boss around?

What Mandy said was true. Money buys property, not people. Possessions, not love. Houses with picket fences, not friendships with Mandy Miller. I guess I'd always known this in the back of my mind. I had certainly heard the saying "money can't buy happiness," but until now, I hadn't really believed it.

But where did my realization get me? The truth was obvious: Mandy Miller was never coming back to the Unicorn Club. I realized that for once in my life, I, Lila Fowler, was going to have to take "no" for an answer.

"Come on, Lila, take a chill pill. Just come with us to Casey's," Jessica said on Monday after school, leaning against my locker.

All day long the Unicorns had taken turns trying to convince me to hang out with them after school. I was still down in the dumps over Mandy. As far as I was concerned, retreating to my bedroom was the only appealing option.

"I haven't changed my mind," I told her, fishing through my locker.

"Maybe you'd actually have a good time," she pleaded.

"I'm not in the mood," I said flatly.

Jessica shook her head in disbelief. "How can you not be in the mood for ice cream?"

"I have all the ice cream I could ever dream to eat in the freezer at home." I slid a couple of books in my backpack.

"But what you don't have at home are Aaron, Peter, Bruce . . . that waitress who loves us so." Jessica cracked herself up.

"I'm not going, Jessica," I told her firmly.

"But you stayed at home all weekend, Lila." Jessica put her hands on her hips. "I think you're sort of blowing this out of proportion. It's not fair. First we lose Mandy, and now it feels like we're losing you. How can we even consider ourselves a club with only three devoted members?"

"You're not losing me," I explained as patiently as possible. "I'm totally devoted to the club. It's just going to take me some time to get over what happened with Mandy. I wouldn't be good company, anyway." I shut my locker. "If you were really a good friend, you'd just leave me alone, OK?"

Jessica sighed as I moved away.

As I walked through the school grounds, my mind was still filled with thoughts about Mandy. I wanted to explain to her that I had learned a valuable lesson, that I would never again try to win someone over by opening my wallet. I wanted to thank her for being the first person who'd ever had the nerve to say those things to me. I wanted to tell her that I understood her decision to break away from the club. But given the fact that she had avoided me all day long, it was going to be a little hard to tell her this face-to-face. I'd have called her on the phone, but that would only give her the opportunity to hang up on me.

Passing through the business district of Sweet Valley, I noticed Adelaide's Flower Shop. I gazed in the window at the vibrant colors. Maybe I could send her an arrangement full of exotic purple flowers? I shook my head, brushing away the thought. She hadn't been too willing to accept anything from me. What would be different about a bouquet of flowers?

Waiting at the intersection of Colby and Sunset, I got another impulse. I could take a different route home. The one that went by the hospital.

"Who are you?" a little boy called out. He was crouched in the corner of his hospital room, making a tower out of building blocks.

I had gathered the nerve to face Mandy and give her my apology in person. Unfortunately, she wasn't where I had expected her to be.

The boy put down his blocks and approached me. I didn't have to ask who he was. It was Randall. I recognized the purple baseball cap he wore—it was Mandy's favorite. She must have given it to him.

"Oh, I, ummm, I'm just looking for Mandy," I stammered. I guess I'm not too relaxed around people who are sick. "I uh, well, I just thought I might find her here."

"But don't you have a name?" he asked.

I shifted my feet. "Oh. Right. Lila. Fowler."

"That's a pretty name. It sounds like Lily Flower. I'm Randall, which I know is kind of a dumb name for a little kid. Randall sounds like an old guy or a grumpy grandpa. Some of the kids at school call me Randy, but my mom doesn't like that."

"Umm," I said. "Really?"

"You know, I wonder if Mandy is short for anything," he continued. "If Randy is short for Randall, then maybe Mandy is short for Mandall."

I giggled and felt myself relax a little. "Who knows," I replied, "maybe she's been hiding it from everybody. Anyway, could you tell me where Mandall is? I mean Mandy."

"What's in it for me?" he asked, climbing onto his bed.

I raised my eyebrows. "What did you have in mind?"

Randall rested his chin in his hands, thinking.

"I could run over to the gift shop," I suggested.

"How about a stuffed animal and a comic book?"

"Nah," he replied.

I looked around the room with a critical eye. "Do you think a pinball machine would fit in here? I could call . . ."

"Play a game of checkers with me," he interrupted.

"Oh, please. I can do better than that for you," I assured him. "I could arrange to get a clown to entertain you for a couple of hours. If I pay him enough, I'm sure he'll play whatever you want."

"But I want *you* to play," he said.

"Me?" I bit my lip. "Really?"

He nodded eagerly.

"You just want me to hang out in here and play checkers?" I asked tentatively.

"You know the rules, don't you?" he replied.

"Well, yeah. But . . ." I checked my watch, even though there was nowhere I had to be.

"Do you have to go somewhere?" He sounded disappointed.

I looked at him closely. I wanted to think of an excuse, but something inside of me suddenly told me not to. "No, I can stay," I replied. "It's fine."

He smiled widely as I sat down in the chair beside his bed.

"I guess this means you get to know where Mandy is," he remarked.

"Yeah. Pay up." I held out my hand.

"She has to do some family thingamajig tonight.

A fifty-year anniversary party for her great-aunt and uncle."

"Fifty years." I whistled. "Wow."

"Oh, I'm going to be married at least that long." Randall took the checkerboard from his bedside table.

"Have any prospects?" I asked, setting up the red and black pieces.

He looked at me strangely. "What's that mean?"

I adjusted my chair so that I could see the board more easily. "I mean, do you know who you'll marry?"

"Of course. Mandy Miller. By the time we're in our twenties, the age difference won't be that big of a deal." Randall turned the board around. "She always lets me be red."

"Fair enough," I said.

Randall moved out his first piece. "So, I guess you're one of Mandy's friends, right?"

I bit my lip as I pushed a piece to a red square. "Well . . . umm . . ."

Randall made a move. "Look, Lily Flower, just 'cause she said she'd be my best friend doesn't mean she can't still be friends with you, too."

"I wish," I said softly.

"Wish what?" he asked.

"Oh, nothing. Nothing. Uh . . . let's see here," I said, staring at the board. With one move I could jump three of his pieces and crown myself. Instead, I pushed my piece the opposite way.

Randall moved a red checker and snagged three of my blacks in the process. He cracked his knuckles. "I'm just getting started."

I looked at him closely. "You know, you seem pretty healthy. Are you sure you're sick? Or is this just a big put-on so you can get girls to play checkers with you?"

"You mean you can't tell I'm a baldy?" he asked me, readjusting his hat.

"So what?" I exclaimed. "It's hip. Don't you know that a bunch of pro basketball players started that trend?"

"But I don't play basketball," he told me.

"Doesn't matter," I said. "You're on the cutting edge of style."

"Maybe when I get better I can learn to play."

"I bet you'll be a natural," I said encouragingly.

"But, it's true that I'm sick. I have surgery tomorrow." He gripped his fists and looked down.

I felt my chest tighten. I'd never had even a little operation. I could only imagine how scared I would be. "What do they have to do?"

"The doctor says it'll make me all better," Randall said. "But I'm still super scared. They have to cut me open."

I winced.

"It wouldn't be so awful, but . . . my mom isn't going to be here, and . . ." His voice trailed off.

"I'm sorry."

"I know she would be here if she could," he continued. "She's driving down tonight just to spend an hour with me. That's like over ten hours of driving for one hour of visiting."

"She must really love you."

Randall nodded. "And if I didn't have Mandy, I don't know what I'd do. My mom and me think she's like an angel."

I nodded. It was amazing to see how much Mandy meant to Randall. "Mandy really is amazing," I said wistfully.

Suddenly, a mischievous grin formed on his face. "You think *she's* amazing? Watch this." He picked up a piece and cruised all the way across the board, removing my four remaining checkers along the way.

"Rematch," I demanded.

As he set up the board, I looked around the room. There were blocks and balls and stuffed animals everywhere. I noticed a drawing of an airplane taped to the wall.

"Did you draw that?" I asked, pointing to the colorful picture.

He looked at it. "Mandy helped. Those are our bloop rints."

I grinned. "You mean your blueprints?"

"Yeah, that's what Mandy calls them. We want to make a plane to take my mom back and forth so she can be here more. So she won't have to drive all the time."

"That'd be awesome."

"It's really impossible," he said. "But that's OK. After my operation I'm only stuck in here for a little longer. Then I get to go home. I'll get to see my dog and go back to school and be with my mom every single day." He slid a checker out.

"I bet you're looking forward to that," I said.

"Except that I'll miss Mandy," he confessed.

I looked at him appreciatively. I guess we had something in common. We both knew how special Mandy was. The difference was that he actually *had* a friendship with her.

Randall tapped my shoulder. "Lily? It's your turn."

"Oh, right. Mmmm." I shook my head and looked at the board, searching for a move that would lock in the win for Randall.

He crowned his piece and went on to beat me in checkers two more times. I'm not crazy about losing at anything, but it was worth it just to see him get so excited.

"The winner gets to pick the next thing to do." He looked at me hopefully. "I mean, if you have to go, it won't hurt my feelings," he said as I cleared away the board.

I did have a history report to write, and Jean Luc was back in town, preparing chicken parmesan for dinner. But I knew Mandy wouldn't have left Randall before his mother arrived. Besides, my dad was still in New York, and I didn't especially want to rush home to an empty house. "I'll hang," I told him.

"Ex-cellent!"

As I looked at Randall, his grinning face, and his purple baseball hat, I realized I had my own reason for staying. It didn't have to do with Mandy's example and it wasn't really about my dad's absence, either. The reason I stayed in the hospital room with Randall was simple—there was nowhere I wanted to be more.

"But," I went on, "there's one condition."

"Name it."

I leaned over and whispered in his ear. "That you don't tell anyone you beat me at checkers three times in a row. It's kind of embarrassing."

"Maybe you're better at crazy eights," he suggested, grabbing a deck of cards on the bedside table.

I grinned as I settled back into the chair. It was the first time since my fight with Mandy that I had been able to have any fun at all.

"I'll deal," I said, shuffling the deck. "Or would you like to?" I asked, offering the cards to Randall.

Nine

"Mandy, you're doing it all wrong," Cecilia said as she watched me put the finishing touches on the anniversary cake. "Let me show you how."

Cecilia took the tube of frosting that I was making pink blobs with and somehow turned them into perfect roses with green stems.

"The guests will be here any minute. I'll bring out the salad. You bring in the flowers," Cecilia instructed as she rushed out of the kitchen with the big bowl.

I glanced at the clock on the stove. It was five o'clock and in a matter of moments the anniversary celebration would begin. But I had something on my mind that was far more important than the party. Visiting hours at the hospital lasted until eight. Somehow I had to make sure I had enough time to get in and see Randall. It was the night before his surgery, and I knew he was counting on a pep talk and a hug from me.

"Why are you so tense?" my mom asked with concern as she came in from the dining room. She was wearing a gingham apron over her nicest black dress.

"You can tell?" I asked hesitantly, drying my hands off on a dish towel.

"Maybe you can put your problems with the Unicorns out of your mind for the night," she said, flicking on the oven light and checking on our dinner.

I leaned against the counter. "That's not it, Mom."

"Is it Randall?" she asked sympathetically.

I nodded. "I just need to make sure that I make it to the hospital before visiting hours are over."

My mom wrinkled her forehead. "I don't want you to count on it, sweetie. Who knows how long dinner will last."

I felt a surge of alarm. "I need to get there, Mom. It's important."

"Honey, what you're doing for Randall is wonderful. You've been with him every day." My mom touched my shoulder affectionately. "But this is your great-aunt and uncle's *fiftieth* wedding anniversary. It's a big deal."

"But his operation is tomorrow," I protested. "He's really afraid. And he's so lonely, Mom."

"I know, Mandy," she replied softly. "And I know how special you are to him. But there's also a whole staff of people at the hospital who can help him to-night. Nurses, candy stripers, other volunteers." She checked the vegetables steaming on the stovetop.

I exhaled with frustration. I wouldn't have felt so upset if I hadn't already missed my daily after-school visit. Not only had I promised my mom that I'd help out with the cooking and cleaning for the party, I had to varnish the photo collage I was mak-ing for my Aunt Holly and Uncle Dan.

"I'm sure Aunt Holly and Uncle Dan will under-stand if I have to leave early, Mom. They know what it's like to have a friend in the hospital," I continued. "And they're really *your* aunt and uncle, not mine."

"Mandy, that's not fair," she admonished.

I gritted my teeth. "I'm sorry, Mom, it's just . . ."

"I know it's important to you to see Randall. And if dinner ends early enough, you can zip over there," she said briskly. "If not, I'm not giving you permission to go. You've been there every single day. Randall will be fine for one night."

"But, Mom," I complained. "I really think—"

"Thanks for bringing in the flowers, Mandy," Cecilia snapped, breezing into the kitchen, taking the arrangement and heading back toward the din-ing room.

"—that it's important he gets some extra sup-port tonight," I said, picking up where I had left off.

Archie whizzed into the kitchen, wearing his fa-vorite outfit: a pinstriped suit made for someone twice his size, a bright orange T-shirt, and a fedora.

My mom sighed. "Oh, Archie, don't you have something else to put on? Just for tonight? You know how Aunt Holly and Uncle Dan feel about the crazy stuff you guys wear. I don't mind but . . ."

The doorbell rang, and my mom turned to me. "You and Cecilia go let the guests in. Archie? Move it or lose it."

I had to admit, the dining room table looked beautiful. My mom had cut roses from the garden for a huge centerpiece, and all the silver had been shined till it sparkled. She had made a beautiful lace tablecloth from a remnant of material she'd found at the fabric store. Mozart played softly in the background. But even the peaceful setting couldn't calm me down. I felt like a nervous wreck, worrying about Randall and how he was holding up in the room all alone.

I could only pray that I was in the company of fast eaters, or that the food was so good, everybody would gobble it right down. And my wish began to come true when the first course whizzed right by.

Cecilia and I cleared the soup bowls as my mom brought in the lamb. At the pace we had established, dinner would be over by seven, giving me plenty of time for a short but sweet visit with Randall. Maybe my aunt and uncle could drop me off at the hospital on their way back home. I would be sure to bring Randall a corner piece from the cake.

But I had forgotten something critical. Aunt

Holly is the slowest eater in the world. The soup went down smoothly, but the lamp chops were another matter. I think it has to do with her dentures or something. Then added to this, the conversation was so lively that hardly any of the other adults made a dent in their food. I was so preoccupied by watching everyone else eat that I forgot about the food in front of me. My eyes wandered from mouth to mouth, watching my mom take a bite of lamb, Uncle Dan have a forkful of peas, and Aunt Holly delicately nibble on a dinner roll. It was *true* torture.

When our guests of honor began reminiscing about the first time they met, I knew a good half hour was down the tubes. Don't get me wrong, I love this story. It's just that tonight of all nights, I didn't want to hear it again. I could feel my whole body tensing up.

"She was working at the five-and-dime," Uncle Dan said.

"He was my best customer," Aunt Holly added, a twinkle in her eye. "But I knew that he had a girl because he would come in and buy a box of chocolates every Friday."

"None of those girls were special to me." Uncle Dan gazed at her adoringly. "But Holly! I would get into her line even if it was the longest one."

I shifted restlessly in my seat.

"It seemed like any other Friday," Aunt Holly went on. "I did the transaction as usual." She turned to me and Cecilia. "An elegant box of candy cost fifty cents back then."

I forced a smile. "Wow," I replied, tapping my foot anxiously underneath the table.

"Anyway," Aunt Holly continued, "when I handed him his change, he looked at me with the silliest expression."

"I said, 'If you'd prefer bittersweet, we could exchange it. This one's for you.' And I handed her back the box." Uncle Dan glowed with pride.

"Did you exchange it?" Cecilia asked, even though she knew the whole story by heart.

"No." Aunt Holly laughed. "I clocked out on my time card."

"We ate the entire box of chocolates on a bench outside," Uncle Dan explained.

"And when he offered me the last milk chocolate caramel? That was the moment I realized I loved him."

They gripped hands tenderly.

"And maybe in honor of that chocolate candy, I should bring out our own chocolate dessert," I suggested quickly. "I'll be right—"

"Mandy, sit down." My mother raised her eyebrows. "Not everyone has finished their dinner yet."

"But they will any minute," I said airily. "I don't want to keep them—"

"Mandy." My mom looked at me knowingly.

"OK, OK." I slumped in my seat.

"Pass the potatoes," Aunt Holly requested.

"I'd like to propose a toast," my mother said, raising her glass of sparkling wine.

A toast? Just when I thought dinner was finally over, she had to propose a toast? I had calculated there was just enough time left to get to the hospital for a good luck hug and a quick conversation.

"I hardly know where to start," my mom began.

Then don't, I wanted to say.

"Aunt Holly, Uncle Dan," my mom said adoringly, "having you in my life is a blessing. And I've always . . ."

As she spoke, all I could think about was Randall. Here were people who had lived long lives full of happy memories. Randall was only seven and fighting for his life. How could I sit here and celebrate when he needed me so much? How could I stay in a room full of family and friends when I knew Randall was in a hospital room all by himself?

"It was a great party, Mom," Cecilia said, spooning leftover rice into a bowl.

"It was, wasn't it?" my mom said pleasantly, wiping crumbs off the counter.

I was at the sink, letting my anger out on the pots and pans and splashing soapy water all over my flowered blouse in the process. By the time toasts, presents, and good-byes were over, it was almost nine. Visiting hours were over. By now Randall was probably tossing and turning under his covers, wondering why I had let him down.

"Thanks for being so helpful," my mom told us. "I couldn't have done all this work without you girls."

"My pleasure, Mom," Cecilia replied.

I grunted to myself and began drying the dishes.

"Mandy? I'm sorry you missed the chance to visit Randall," my mom apologized.

I pretended I couldn't hear her over the clatter of the pots and pans.

When I finally finished my cleanup responsibilities, I dashed up to my room. I flopped on my bed and thought about how I had felt before my own operation last year. It was the scariest night of my life. I'd never had surgery before, not even a tonsillectomy, or for a broken arm or stitches. I was terrified that I might never wake up, never live to see the sunshine the next day. But my mom had been there to hold my hand and tell me that it would be OK. She had waited by my bedside until I'd fallen asleep and she was the first person I saw when I'd opened my eyes the next morning. Thinking back, I know that it was her support more than anything else that got me through the ordeal.

How would Randall be able to handle the fear by himself? I'd been twelve when I had my operation—he was only seven. Some kids his age are still afraid of the dark. How would he make it through something this major on his own?

Of course, I felt pretty alone, too. But who could I call?

I looked at the list of phone numbers that I had tacked to my bulletin board over the years. Kimberly Haver. Ellen Riteman. Lila Fowler. When

Lila was still a friend, she would have been a perfect listener. She may not have been able to understand what I was going through with Randall, but she would have found a way to take my mind off of things by bringing up boys or clothes or the latest Johnny Buck movie. But at this point, Lila was the last person in the world I would call. I would sooner open up to a stranger than to Lila Fowler.

My eyes scanned the other numbers scattered on the board. There had to be someone I could turn to. Evie Kim? I hadn't really talked to her in weeks. Mary Wallace? I wouldn't feel comfortable opening up to her. Maria Slater? We hadn't spoken on the phone in such a long time that if I said it was Mandy calling, she'd probably ask, "Mandy who?" Aaron Dallas? Compassion from a boy who laughs at news footage of fires and floods? I don't think so.

I finally focused on the slip that read Jessica and Elizabeth Wakefield. Before things had changed, Jessica was the first friend I would have phoned. She was my confidante, my right-hand man. She always had a way of looking at any situation from a totally weird but cool perspective. Well, so much for listening to Jessica's funny takes on things. Our friendship was over.

Out of all the names, and all the students at Sweet Valley Middle School, the only person I still felt comfortable calling was Elizabeth. Elizabeth and I go way back, and I know she doesn't hold a grudge against me for not choosing the Angels. But what if

Jessica answered the phone? What would I say? I'd be so tongue-tied, I'd probably hang up on her.

I grabbed a stuffed turtle from my bed and hugged it to my chest. I had to face the obvious: I didn't have anyone to turn to. My only friend was alone in a hospital room, wondering how I could have let him down.

Ten

"All right, Randall, what would you rather learn about? Getting a base tan before hitting the beach, zapping zits with homemade treatments, or how to perfect the art of flirting?"

It was after visiting hours, but I was still hanging out with Randall. I'd finally convinced Nurse Talkington to give me special permission to stay. Randall's mother wasn't expected until nine or so, and I didn't want to leave him alone the night before his big surgery.

After Randall creamed me in our crazy eights tournament, clobbered me in tic-tac-toe and drew my portrait with crayons, he asked me to read him a story. But I couldn't find a good kid's book anywhere. Randall had lent all of his to a little girl down the hall, and Nurse Talkington couldn't find anything in the supply room. After rummaging through the magazine racks in the lobby, I had resorted to the latest issue of *Teen Talk* for our bedtime reading material.

"Oh, and there's an up close in person article about Johnny Buck," I went on, scanning the rest of the table of contents.

"Who's he?" Randall asked.

"Only like the greatest actor, musician, babe of all times," I explained.

Randall tapped his finger on his chin. "Forget about bucky boy. I don't care much about getting a tan. I think I'm already a pretty good flirt for a seven-year-old. I guess I'd rather learn about zits, since I don't really know what they are."

"OK, zits it is," I said, flipping to the page where the article began. "'From Pizza Face to Peachy Face: How to Zap Zits Permanently.'" I held up a the photograph of a blond teenager before and after the home treatment.

"Looks like it works," he said, "but she's still not as pretty as Mandy."

I felt a knot in my stomach. For the last hour I'd managed to forget about Mandy and how I'd messed up our friendship. Even the mention of her name made me feel sad again.

"What's the matter, Lily Flower?" Randall asked, leaning toward me.

I cleared my throat. "Nothing. Nothing. Really."

Randall studied me. "It's 'cause you're a girl,

huh? I've seen it happen to Mandy and my mom, too. You just get upset for no reason."

I managed a smile. "Yeah, girls are silly that way, I guess. Now let's learn about zapping zits." I cleared my throat again and began to read. " 'One of the most common traumas in the teen years is the sudden emergence of acne. What once was clear childhood skin has become overnight covered with blemishes and bumps.' "

Randall rubbed his palm over his cheek. "I guess I have what they call 'clear childhood skin.' "

I touched his soft cheek. "Ooooh. Very smooth. Are you sure you don't already know about these methods?"

He giggled. "They're my beauty secret."

I laughed. "Well, here are some more secrets for you." I looked at the article once again. "Before you waste time and money at the drugstore for antiseptics and lotions, see if your refrigerator holds some of the best ingredients for this battle of the bumps. Eggs, mayonnaise, avocado—"

"Yuck!" Randall hollered. "That's disgusting. They really think someone would use that gunk?"

"A small price to pay for a perfect complexion," I told him. "Maybe I'll try out their recipe tomorrow. Not that I have any zits, of course." I flung my hair over my shoulder. "Just a preventative measure."

"Maybe you should buy a bag of tortilla chips and see if it tastes yummy as a dip, too," he suggested.

Randall let out snorts of laughter, and I giggled so hard that my stomach hurt.

"If it's good, I'll bring you the leftovers," I joked.

"Randall?" a soft voice called out.

I turned around and saw a woman standing in the doorway. Her face seemed tight with tension, and her hair was messy. I knew without asking. It was Randall's mother.

"Mommy! You made it!" he screamed joyfully.

"You bet," she said, stepping inside.

I smiled at her. "I'm Lila."

"She stinks at games, but she's pretty fun to be around anyway," Randall told her. "She's kept me company all night long."

"Nurse Talkington already told me," she replied appreciatively. "It's wonderful of you to be here, Lila."

I stood up so she could take the chair by Randall's bedside.

"So how's my baby boy holding up?" she asked, running her pointer finger along the crease in his arm.

"Good," he said with determination.

To tell you the truth, Randall seemed fine. He really didn't seem freaked out about tomorrow's operation. It was his mother who looked like the stress case. I know how to read people well enough to tell you that Mrs. Boyer was trying to act more relaxed than she was. I couldn't blame her. Here was her only son, about to go in for the operation of his life, and she only had an hour to spend with him.

"Since you're already here, why can't you just stay, Mom?" he asked.

"I wish I could, sweetie, but remember what I told you?" she answered patiently. "I can't afford to miss another day of work. Now, we've only got an hour to be together, so let's make it nice, OK? Let's not talk about the things that are out of our control."

"Just stay the night," he pleaded. "You can leave super early in the morning. Couldn't you be just an hour late for work or something?"

"I thought of that, sweetie, I did. But it's impossible. Tomorrow they're doing road construction on the five freeway and they're rerouting traffic. I'd never make it back." She looked down at her hands.

"If only Mandy and I could have had our plane ready," Randall said, staring at his drawing on the wall.

Plane? I thought suddenly. Would a plane really solve their problems?

My mind began whirring. My dad has a private plane that sits in the hangar at the Sweet Valley Airport. More than anything I wanted to offer its use to Mrs. Boyer. I wanted to call Mr. Winkler, our pilot, and arrange for him to take her home first thing in the morning and bring her back immediately after work. But I hesitated. Mandy had shown me how out of line it was to go throwing my money around and buying outrageous presents for people. I didn't want to do that again. I didn't want to insult Randall and his mom.

"Well, you *do* make some pretty nice paper airplanes," Mrs. Boyer told Randall. "And if I could, I'd sit on its little wings and let it whisk me up the coast."

"I don't know, Mom, that might not be too safe," Randall warned her.

Mrs. Boyer sighed and stroked Randall's forehead. "I know it's not the same, Randall, but I hope you can understand that I'll be with you in spirit."

I hugged my elbows, watching them hopefully. Maybe knowing how much his mom loved him would be enough to get Randall through the night. And tomorrow I would come back, Mandy would be here, and I knew the nurses and doctors would give him special attention, too. But there was no denying that the ordeal would be easier to handle if his mother was around.

How could I just stand there silently when I knew there was something I could do? What's the point of having money if you don't share the wealth every once in a while?

I took a deep breath. "Don't drive home tonight," I told Randall's mom.

Randall and Mrs. Boyer looked at me curiously.

"You can come stay with me," I offered. "We have nine extra bedrooms."

Mrs. Boyer smiled softly. "Oh, Lila, that's such a kind offer, but . . . I, I still have to be at work in the morning."

"I can get you there," I insisted.

She smiled. "That's very kind of you, but . . ."

"I'm serious," I went on excitedly. "I mean, I'll have to call and get the OK from my dad, but we have a private plane and a pilot and everything. He could fly you home in the morning, wait while you're at work, and fly you back down so you're here when Randall comes out of surgery."

Randall's eyes were wide with surprise. "You have your own jet?"

I glanced at the picture on the wall. "Well, it's not nearly as cool as the one you and Mandy designed, but it does the job."

Mrs. Boyer fidgeted with the strap of her purse. "Lila, look, it's a very kind offer, really, I'm amazed. But I don't think I'm comfortable accepting this. We just barely met, we . . ."

"No offense, Mrs. Boyer, but it's not for you. It's for Randall." Randall and I met eyes. "Knowing that you'll be waiting for him when he comes out of surgery will make it so much easier on him."

She exhaled. "I, well . . . I . . ."

"Look, I have the perfect plan," I went on. "Our chauffeur will take you from my house to the hospital first thing in the morning. You can spend some time with Randall and then fly directly to work."

"Please, Mom?" Randall asked hopefully. "Please?"

Mrs. Boyer pursed her lips. "Well, it's a hard offer to turn down."

"So don't," I urged.

"Well . . ." Mrs. Boyer looked from me to Randall and back. Then a smile spread over her face. "As long as you get approval from your father first, you've got a deal."

"I'll be right back," I said, rushing for the pay phone down the hall. But I knew the arrangements were already a done deal. In business, my dad knows how to say no. But he's never been able to say it to me. And he wouldn't make tonight a first. Especially when I knew that the three-hour time difference made it past midnight in New York, and I would be catching him in a groggy, but agreeable, mood.

Eleven

I watched the second hand on the wall clock in my history class. Eleven . . . ten . . . nine . . . I counted off the seconds until the bell would ring and I'd take off to see Randall. Three . . . two . . . one! I grabbed my notebook, sprang up, and started making my way out of the classroom.

"Mandy," I heard a voice call out.

I turned around.

"Mandy?" My history teacher, Mrs. Morrison, repeated in her stern voice. "Aren't you forgetting something?"

I gulped. "Me?"

Why, of all days, had I been singled out of the crowd? Was it for spacing out during her lecture? For coming in a mere few seconds after the second bell?

She stood up from behind her desk. "Today is

the day we scheduled your makeup test."

I gasped. "My makeup test?"

I had missed a test a couple weeks back when I was home with the flu and had managed to put off taking the makeup twice already.

"It's the last day before mid-term report cards need to be filed, so no excuse will work this time," she told me.

"But I . . . I . . . umm . . ." I stammered. I hadn't prepared for the test, but that was the least of my worries. Randall was due out of surgery any moment, and the thought of his returning to an empty hospital room was too horrible even to think about. After missing our visit last night, I had to be there for him. I couldn't let him down again. "Couldn't I . . . just . . . come back in a couple of hours and take it?"

Mrs. Morrison placed the test on my desk. "This is on my time, Mandy," she said firmly, pointing at the answer sheet. "I'm not about to wait around for you to spend a couple of hours stuffing or cramming, or whatever it is you kids call it."

I exhaled with frustration. "But . . ."

"The sooner you finish, the sooner we both get to leave," she said, returning to her desk. "I suggest you start now before I deduct points from your overall score."

I clenched my teeth. There was no way out. I pulled a pencil from my backpack, took my seat, and began the test.

I don't know how it happened, but my hand

managed to flow across the sheet and circle the answers. I made a few educated guesses about the Battle of Little Bighorn and the main accomplishments during Andrew Johnson's presidency, finishing the test as quickly as possible.

As I dashed up to Mrs. Morrison with my completed exam, I glanced at the clock. It was three-fifteen. If I ran all the way to the hospital, I could still be the face that Randall awoke to.

"Don't they teach you kids to read in school these days?" a big burly bearded man in a hard hat and construction garb yelled at me.

I was taking the shortcut to the hospital when I'd run into orange cones and a big sign that read ROAD CONSTRUCTION/USE ALTERNATE ROUTES. Pressed for time, I had decided to try to sneak past the barriers.

"Well, of course, I can read, but I'm in a . . ."

"Then what's the problem?" he asked, pointing to the orange sign. "You want to get smacked by flying concrete, or run over by a tractor?"

"Can I borrow your hard hat?" I asked hopefully. "I'll bring it back, I'll . . ."

He crossed his arms over his stomach and shook his head.

"OK. I'm leaving," I said with frustration, quickly turning around.

"Excuse me? Ma'am, uh, excuse me?" I said with all the patience I could muster up.

A woman who was walking about ten small terriers stepped aside so that I could pass her.

The road construction wasn't the end of my problems. Because everything was rerouted off of Colby, one of the main thruways in town, the alternate route to the hospital was filled with a ton of foot traffic. There were women pushing strollers, businesspeople mingling, and street carts hogging the sidewalk.

Finally I made it to the hospital steps—and tripped on my way up. My knee killed me, but I didn't bother to see if I had skinned it. The pain of having let Randall down was far worse than a little nick on my leg.

I was panting by the time I reached Randall's room. I took two steps in and gasped. "Mrs. Boyer?" I whispered, catching my breath.

Mrs. Boyer was sitting by Randall's side, holding his hand as he slept. When she saw me, she put her finger over her mouth and motioned to the hallway.

"He woke up for a few minutes after the operation and fell right back asleep," Mrs. Boyer said once we were outside the room. "The doctors say he'll be out for a little longer while the anesthesia wears off."

I had so many questions, I didn't know where to begin. "So he's OK? It went well? What did Dr. Baron say?" I asked breathlessly.

"Went without a glitch," she told me, smiling faintly.

I felt all the tension drain out of me. "Thank goodness!"

"Randall asked for you when he woke up," she said.

I sighed sadly. "You wouldn't believe what I went through to get here. I'm sorry that I had to let him down."

Mrs. Boyer patted my shoulder affectionately. "You've been such an integral part of his entire hospital stay. Randall knows that you'd have been here if you could have."

Hearing that from Mrs. Boyer made me feel much better. It lifted some of the guilt and disappointment I had been feeling since yesterday. And with Mrs. Boyer here, I knew that it wasn't nearly as important for me to be. "But I still don't understand something," I said. "How did you ever manage to be here yourself?"

Mrs. Boyer looked at me curiously. "I thought Lila would have told you at school."

"Lila?" I repeated.

Mrs. Boyer smiled widely. "She was a savior."

"You mean Lila . . . *Fowler*?" I asked hesitantly.

Mrs. Boyer nodded admiringly. "Of course, I would have expected your friends to be as giving and caring as you are."

I frowned. Giving and caring were not adjectives that people usually used to describe the prima donna herself. "You're sure this was Lila Fowler? I mean, did she have bouncy brown hair and perfect teeth and diamond stud . . ."

"Earrings?" Mrs. Boyer said, completing my sentence. "And she just bubbles over with warmth."

Warmth? Lila Fowler isn't warm to anyone unless she's trying to get something out of them—and even then it's a cold kind of warmth. "Wh-what did she do?" I asked, trying to sound pleasant.

Mrs. Boyer adjusted her purse on her shoulder. "Well, she was here yesterday when I drove in from Danville, and—"

"Here? In *this* hospital?" I broke in. "Doing what?"

Mrs. Boyer raised her eyebrows. "Randall told me you were busy with a relative's party or something, so I just assumed that you'd asked Lila to come in your place."

I shook my head. "Umm, not exactly."

"Well, she was wonderful." Mrs. Boyer beamed. "I expected to find Randall in a bundle of nerves the night before the operation, but when I came in, he and Lila were laughing and cracking jokes."

Lila hanging out with a seven-year-old? This was too much to be believed. "Really?" I replied.

Mrs. Boyer peered back in through the window to check on Randall. "But even more important than her company, Lila made it possible for me to be here today."

I brushed my hair off my forehead, still stumped. "I thought you had to be at work."

"I went," she answered triumphantly. "I slept at Lila's house last night. After I visited with Randall this morning, her private plane flew me straight to work and back here afterward."

I couldn't believe my ears. Randall had gotten his super-fast jet after all. In a way, Lila had made his dream come true.

But I was still confused. Why had she done it? What was her motive? What did she stand to gain? "Wh-what, I, well, how, I mean . . . ?" I bit my lip. I couldn't just come straight out and ask Mrs. Boyer why she thought Lila would have done it for her. "How did it all work out?" I asked instead.

"I had to leave work a little early, and believe me it took a lot of guts to ask my boss to let me off," she explained, "but the plane took me back down so I could be here when Randall woke up after his surgery."

"Lila arranged all that for you?" I asked.

"You know, I was really reluctant about taking her offer," she mused, "but I'm so glad I did. It made the world of difference to Randall." She frowned a little. "Mandy, are you all right? You look like you might faint."

"Uh—yeah, I'm fine," I said quickly, even though *fine* wasn't exactly the word for what I was feeling. In fact, I didn't know *what* I was feeling. But I did know that I was having a hard time seeing what Lila did as anything but wonderful. And who cared why she did it? The point was that it had helped Randall. And she didn't even try to impress me by telling me about it. Could she have actually done something out of the goodness of her heart? "I . . . I guess Lila can be really generous," I admitted.

"And she obviously has such a sensible way of sharing her wealth. I mean, wouldn't that be the pleasure of being rich? Being able to help others?" Mrs. Boyer went on. "It's the kindest thing that anyone's ever done for me." She dabbed a tear from the corner of her eye.

I felt myself getting choked up, too. It was as if Lila had made a complete turnaround. She had milked her resources for the right reason and in the right way. And it wasn't just the plane ride or letting Mrs. Boyer stay the night that touched me; it was the fact that Lila had been here with Randall. The whole time that I was worried about him being in the room alone, he was goofing around with Lila.

"She was here when he woke up from surgery," Mrs. Boyer added. "You just missed her."

"She was?" I replied.

"What a wonderful friend you have," Mrs. Boyer said tearfully. "When times get rough, there's nothing more important than having a good friend to lean on."

I nodded slowly. Suddenly my mind flashed back in time. To times when Lila and the other Unicorns had been just that—good friends to lean on.

"She was here for me, too. When I was sick," I said thoughtfully. "That's when we became friends."

I would never forget the way the Unicorns had cared for me when I had cancer. I would never be able to thank them enough for buying me the wig that made going back to school seem safe.

And there were other things, too. One time the Unicorns came over to help repaint our old shabby furniture and give my house a face-lift. I thought about how caring Lila had been with Ellie McMillan, a little girl at the child care center, and her unemployed mom. She'd helped Mrs. McMillan back on her feet by getting her a job at Fowler Enterprises. I also remembered how awesome she was around the other kids at the center. One day she treated them all to a day at the zoo, something they could never have afforded on their own.

Maybe I had been too harsh on Lila. I had been noticing the negative without taking stock of the positive. Lila still shouldn't have tried to buy me back into the club the way she had, but it didn't cancel out every great thing she'd ever done, either. Maybe she'd learned a lesson. And maybe if I were as rich as she, I'd try something sneaky myself.

I looked at Mrs. Boyer appreciatively. "Thank you, Mrs. Boyer."

"Me?" she asked. "I should be thanking you. For everything you've done for Randall and for me, and—"

"But you did something for me, too," I explained with a smile. "You helped me remember something."

"I did?" Mrs. Boyer leaned toward me. "What?"

"How great my friends are."

* * *

When I ran into Casey's, the Unicorns were hanging out at the regular booth. I was about to rush over to them when I remembered something. Last time we saw each other, we'd had a major blowup. I was embarrassed about the way I had acted at the hospital. What if they were mad or unforgiving? Lila has been known to hold a grudge against people who put her down.

And even if they did forgive me, what did I want from them, anyway? Was it just their friendship? Or was it full-fledged membership in the Unicorn Club? I wasn't ready to make that kind of decision. I slipped into a booth a few slots over from them and ducked down to make sure they couldn't see me. I needed some time to psych myself up and to figure out what move to make.

"It was so great hanging out with Randall," Lila was saying.

I sucked in my breath, hearing Lila's words. I hadn't intended to eavesdrop, but it was irresistible.

"He's only like half our age, but he's really cool," Lila went on. "Oh, and he thought up this perfect nickname for me. Lily Flower. Feel free to use it, too."

I stifled my laughter.

"You expect us to call you Lily Flower?" Kimberly scoffed.

"Why not?" Lila asked. "It suits me perfectly—my petal-soft complexion, my naturally sweet scent . . ."

"I think I'll stick with Lila," Jessica said.

"Fine," Lila replied. "I guess it's more special if he's the only one who uses it."

"Lily? Lily," Ellen said thoughtfully. "I like it, Lily."

"And if you guys want a flowerlike complexion like mine, you can try this great facial treatment that Randall and I read about," Lila continued. "We should all do it together at the next Unicorn meeting."

"Not that stupid thing in *Teen Talk*?" Jessica said angrily. "I already tried it. It *gave* me zits!"

"Poor baby," Kimberly said with a giggle.

"Randall sounds really adorable," Ellen said. "Can we go to the hospital later?"

"Not today. He's really worn out from the surgery," Lila answered authoritatively. "The doctor said he'll be groggy from the anesthetic for the next day or so. But he won't check out for another couple of weeks. There are still a few rounds of chemotherapy and radiation."

I smiled to myself. It was as if Lila had become a nurse overnight. She knew all the details of Randall's treatment. And she obviously really cared about him.

Kimberly twirled her hair around her finger. "So let's go visit him tomorrow. I'm a master checkers player, you know."

"Kimberly, the point is to let him win. Get it? It makes him feel good." Lila rolled her eyes.

Lila lose at something on purpose? This was a lot to digest.

"I hope Mandy doesn't mind us all going over to be with him," Jessica remarked. "I wouldn't want her to think we were trying to one up her or take his attention away."

Mind? I thought. Are they kidding? With all the attention the Unicorns could provide, Randall was guaranteed a speedy recovery.

"You know, I think this club should start doing more things for other people," Lila said, sitting up straight in her seat.

"The Angels are cataloging books at the library, Lila," Jessica teased. "They could probably use some help."

"Laugh if you want, but volunteerism is very p.c.," Lila retorted.

"What's that?" Ellen asked.

"Politically correct," Lila answered. "And it's very hip to donate your time to good causes. Like Johnny Buck volunteers at a homeless shelter every Thanksgiving. I've seen pictures of him giving turkey and stuffing to all these poor people."

"Really? Let's pretend we're homeless and go next year," Ellen suggested.

"Ellen! That's totally rude," Kimberly scolded.

Jessica turned to Lila. "Speaking of Johnny Buck, are you still up for seeing *Terminal Bliss*, or will you be too busy being p.c.?"

"Oh, please. I haven't lost my mind," Lila told

her with a sniff. "But playing a little checkers with a seven-year-old who's got cancer never hurt anyone. Of course, I never would have known that if I hadn't stumbled into Randall on my way to apologize to Mandy."

So that's how she had ended up at the hospital. She had come by to tell me she was sorry. Suddenly, I felt weirdly glad I hadn't made it there. This way Lila had had a chance to bond with Randall, Randall had made a new friend—and I got to see how wonderful Lila could be.

Lila sighed. "That's the one thing that really bums me out. We really blew it with Mandy. It was so ridiculous of me to buy that house. I mean, just being there for Randall was more important than any presents I could have bought him." She smiled mischievously. "Although he did love the pocket video game, the basketball, and the high-tops I gave him when he woke up from his surgery."

"Yeah, I'm so sure," Kimberly said with a giggle.

Lila exhaled and looked down. "But trying to win Mandy over with material things was a huge mistake."

I perked up in my seat. Lila had finally seen the light—that money can only get you so far in life. And as I listened to the girls in the booth straight ahead, I realized that I, too, wanted something that money couldn't buy. It was more valuable than any possession I could ever own. More meaningful than something that comes from a store. Even more special than a handmade gift. What I wanted, more than anything in the world, was to be back in the Unicorn Club.

"Huge mistake," Ellen agreed. "I knew it all along."

"Well, thanks a lot for stopping me!" Lila snapped. "We could have avoided this whole mess. We could have just talked to her and told her how we really feel about her."

"Mandy was so mad at us," Jessica said sadly. "She'll probably never speak to us again."

I didn't need to hear any more. I popped out of the booth and rushed to their table. "Says who?" I said.

"Mandy!" Jessica cried as I planted myself in front of them.

"Mandy!" Lila echoed, clutching the table.

Ellen and Kimberly looked at me in alarm.

I smiled at them. "Looking for a new member?" I asked confidently.

"Are you joking?" Kimberly replied. "I thought you thought we were conniving and . . ."

"She thinks *Lila's* conniving," Ellen said seriously. "She never really said anything bad about the rest of us."

Lila rolled her eyes at Ellen.

"I don't know *what* you're talking about," I told them. "I heard that the Unicorn Club is a really amazing group. Rumor is, that they're incredibly diverse and pretty fun to hang around with. By the way, I'm Mandy Miller."

A smile grew on Lila's face. "You really want to

come back to the Unicorns?" she asked hopefully.

I nodded vigorously.

"Well, we're very exclusive," Lila teased.

I looked at Jessica, Ellen, Kimberly, and finally at Lila. "So am I," I replied seriously.

"Then welcome back!" Jessica squealed.

"Really?" I said with excitement, scooting into the booth next to Lila. "After all those things I yelled at you in the hospital, I thought you might never forgive me."

"You might have a career as a trial lawyer," Lila said proudly. "It's a true talent to be able to tell someone off like that."

"Really," Jessica concurred. "Next time I'm having it out with Elizabeth, maybe you can give me some pointers."

"I'm psyched, Mandy, but I still don't understand," Kimberly said. "What made you change your mind?"

"Lila did." I looked at Lila thoughtfully. "I was just at the hospital and I talked to Mrs. Boyer. What Lila did for Randall . . ."

"It was not *that* big a deal," Lila said modestly. "It was actually fun. Kind of rewarding."

"Exactly," I replied. "It reminded me of all the wonderful, thoughtful things the group has done. It reminded me why I used to be proud to be a Unicorn."

"There are a few things you should know before you agree to officially rejoin the club," Ellen said authoritatively. "You should know that I'm president now."

"That's only *one* thing, Ellen," Kimberly teased her.

"I know, I'm going to think of two others." Ellen frowned in concentration for a moment. "OK. The club never felt the same without you. That's two. And three? This calls for a celebration!" she yelled, signaling over the waitress.

The waitress reluctantly approached our table. "Oh, no. I remember the five of you."

The five of you? It sounded nice. "The five of us," I repeated softly, looking around at my friends. After all the turmoil that had started at the beginning of the year, the Unicorn Club was finally back in full force.

"Are you sure you're ready?" the waitress asked wearily, pulling out her pad.

"It's a simple order," Lila promised. "A round of triple fudge brownie explosions!"

"Just don't dare to try and pay for mine," I said.

Lila smiled smugly. "I wasn't about to offer."

"I'm soooo glad you're a Unicorn again," Jessica said, linking her arm through mine and beginning to skip. We were walking part of the way home together after Casey's. The other Unicorns had already gone their separate ways.

"Me, too," I said happily. "Only—"

"Only what?" Jessica asked, stopping suddenly.

"Well, it'll be tough to tell the Angels that I've

made a final decision," I sighed. "I mean, they really are pretty great." Something just occurred to me. "Hey, maybe we could hang out with them sometimes as a group." I looked at her cautiously. "I hope there's not too much bad blood between the Angels and the Unicorns. . . ."

"I don't know, Mandy," Jessica said skeptically. "I mean, I love my sister and everything, but as a general rule I'd say you should never cross an Angel with a Unicorn. You never know what will happen."

What happens when you cross an Angel with a Unicorn? Find out in THE UNICORN CLUB #11, **Angels Keep Out**.

SIGN UP FOR THE SWEET VALLEY HIGH® FAN CLUB!

Hey, girls! Get all the gossip on Sweet Valley High's® most popular teenagers when you join our fantastic Fan Club! As a member, you'll get all of this really cool stuff:

- Membership Card with your own personal Fan Club ID number
- A Sweet Valley High® Secret Treasure Box
- Sweet Valley High® Stationery
- Official Fan Club Pencil (for secret note writing!)
- Three Bookmarks
- A "Members Only" Door Hanger
- Two Skeins of J. & P. Coats® Embroidery Floss with flower barrette instruction leaflet
- Two editions of *The Oracle* newsletter
- Plus exclusive Sweet Valley High® product offers, special savings, contests, and much more!

Be the first to find out what Jessica & Elizabeth Wakefield are up to by joining the Sweet Valley High® Fan Club for the one-year membership fee of only $6.25 each for U.S. residents, $8.25 for Canadian residents (U.S. currency). Includes shipping & handling.

Send a check or money order (do not send cash) made payable to "Sweet Valley High® Fan Club" along with this form to:

SWEET VALLEY HIGH® FAN CLUB, BOX 3919-B, SCHAUMBURG, IL 60168-3919

NAME_____
(Please print clearly)

ADDRESS_____

CITY_____ STATE_____ ZIP_____
(Required)

AGE_____BIRTHDAY_____ /_____ /_____